Date Due

MAR 17 1995			

BRODART, INC.   Cat. No. 23 233   Printed in U.S.A.

SUMMA PUBLICATIONS, INC.

Thomas M. Hines
Publisher

Norris J. Lacy
Editor-in-Chief

Editorial Board

Benjamin F. Bart
University of Pittsburgh

William Berg
University of Wisconsin

Germaine Brée
Wake Forest University

Michael Cartwright
McGill University

Hugh M. Davidson
University of Virginia

Wallace Fowlie
Duke University (Emeritus)

James Hamilton
University of Cincinnati

Freeman G. Henry
University of South Carolina

Edouard Morot-Sir
*University of North Carolina
Chapel Hill*

Jerry C. Nash
University of New Orleans

Ronald W. Tobin
*University of California
Santa Barbara*

Philip A. Wadsworth
University of South Carolina (Emeritus)

ORDERS:
Box 20725
Birmingham, AL 35216

EDITORIAL ADDRESS:
1904 Countryside
Lawrence, KS 66044

Thresholds: A Study of Proust

Thresholds: A Study of Proust

by

Gerda R. Blumenthal

SUMMA PUBLICATIONS
Birmingham, Alabama
1984

Copyright 1984
Summa Publications, Inc.
ISBN 0-917786-06-8

Printed in the United States of America

PQ
2631
.R63
Z544
1984

In memory of
A.C.R.

Acknowledgments

Beyond the dozen or so critics whose far-reaching insights into Proust's fictional universe have over the years become so integral a part of my own reading of the texts that I could not say now where their readings end and mine begins, a number of friends, colleagues and students were instrumental in helping me to clarify the perspectives developed in this essay. My greatest debts are to Marjorie Perloff, friend and former colleague, of the University of Southern California, Renée Riese Hubert of Irvine, Albert Sonnenfeld of Princeton, Virgil Nemoianu, colleague and director of the Comparative Literature Program at the Catholic University of America, and Linda Cades of the University of Maryland, all of whom read the manuscript at various stages and offered invaluable advice. I am grateful to Catholic University for freeing me to work on this study by granting me a sabbatical leave of absence and a generous research award. I thank Random House for graciously granting me permission to quote from the English version of Proust's novel, *Remembrance of Things Past*.

CONTENTS

Introduction i

I. Pre-texts
   1. Reading: Reality and Metaphor 1
   2. Threshold Creations 13
   3. "A Ray of Sunshine" 27

II. The Text: Two-in-One
   4. A Book of Hours 45
   5. A Book of Questions 57

III. Beyond the Text
   6. Beyond the Text 71

Conclusion 79

Notes 85

Introduction

Like all great works, *A la recherche du temps perdu* remains elusive. Enriched, and in a sense transformed, by every critical perspective which has shed new light on it, it keeps engaging each reader anew, eliciting from him a deciphering which is unlikely to coincide fully with those of previous readers, including himself, since after all each time he rereads its volumes he himself is no longer the same but a new reader.

Already the cycle's metamorphoses - from social chronicle of the belle époque through, most recently, favorite text for deconstructive readings - have been so many and so striking that a present-day reader may well wonder whether it has remained the same book. The answer implicit in the novel itself is significantly twofold. If, as the narrator puts it to his own prospective reader, and as Proust had earlier explained in his Ruskin essay, "Sur la lecture,"[1] a book's essential mission is not to become an immutable cult object and end in itself, but rather to "incite" its reader to become in his turn a decipherer of the truths of life and of art, then clearly *A la recherche* has not remained the same, nor will it as long as it will be read. Yet in another and equally Proustian sense it has of course remained the same. What successive readers have gleaned from it through the particular grids they placed on it or, to use the narrator's metaphor, by means of their own, individually adjusted glasses or optical instruments, the text itself continues to hold together in a totality which always remains just out of grasp. Eluding its would-be captors, it is and remains a unique, self-contained creation. Each new reading of it, spawned by the mutually reinforcing powers of the novel to remagnetize the world for its reader and of successive readings to remagnetize the novel, seeks to capture a fresh sense of the whole, only to have to disclose in its turn the distance which separates its own wholeness from that of the text.

So it must of course be with the present essay, which is as partial in what it leaves unaccounted for in *A la recherche* as in what, conversely, it sets out to bring into clearer view. The latter is the crucial interplay which unfolds in *A la recherche* between a book to come, still to be written by the cycle's end, in and through which the narrator and book's putative writer expects the opaque, fragmented text of his life to be revealed in its essential meaning, and Marcel Proust's own novel, *A la recherche du temps perdu*, which tells the tale of that elusive book.

In the narrator's meditation on his book, which he addresses to his own prospective reader in the cycle's final "Matinée" chapter, the polar opposition between the book's power to bear witness to another, truer world, which it embodies in transparent figural constellations, and the blindness and falseness of the world of the here and now which befuddles the truth-reader's senses and judgment as each new season thrusts all preceding ones into deeper oblivion, appears absolute. And, inseparable from it, so does the antithesis between the spectral figure of the narrator who, upon the sudden eruption in his consciousness of the powers of the involuntary memory, is ready to decipher and, thereby, redeem his life in its totality, and his prior self, the novel's errant hero who, right up to the moment of conversion, has remained caught up in "that perpetual error which is precisely 'life.' "[2]

That the tale is structured by this fundamental antithesis, the most crucial corollary of which is the opposition between the deadly flow of actual time which engulfs all things, and the lifesaving power of reminiscence in the form of the involuntary memory, needs no reiteration. The symmetry created by the tale between the tragic futility of the world, in particular the world of Proust's own experience, and the book's power to redeem that futility, lends the cycle the completeness of a salvation drama. But both within that very structure which appears so closed, yet is so open in its mysterious beginning and in its ending which is but a new beginning, and in the unfolding of the actual tale, a different perspective is opened up. It reveals a fluid realm of thresholds in which the polar opposition between life and the book, and all its corollaries, are transformed into dynamic relationships of kinship and exchange.

The following pages are designed to draw to the fore the extraordinarily rich middle register in which this interplay can be seen working itself out. As the narrative progressively "deciphers" the multiple sketches from life which its hero's "inner sketchbook" has preserved as pre-texts from which he has throughout the cycle been learning the art of reading, in its metaphoric sense of deciphering the hidden truth of things, that art reveals itself to be one of unexpected complexity and is by no means confined to the narrator alone. In defiance of the narrator's dream and the tale's ostensible assertions, what the narrative reveals is, first, that a book cannot but fail in its mission if that mission is to decipher life in all its hidden truth. Secondly, it abounds in signals that life itself is far from totally blind. The fictional universe of *A la recherche* encompasses a spectrum of "readings" that spans the distance between the ostensible blindness of its hero and the would-be orphic deciphering powers of that hero turned narrator, and in which both exchange signals not only with one another, but with a striking array of other "readers." It extends from non-reading to misreading, to the partial divinations of instinct, from there, through a crucial metaphoric extension, to the multiple arts of "translation," and finally to reading as ideally envisioned by the narrator and to be embodied in his book to come. Which prompts the attention of the reader of *A la recherche* to shift from the elusive book in the tale back to the narrative which tells it. Significantly, this narrative constitutes only partly the ideally invoked uncovering of hidden truths. The counterpart of its decipherings throughout the cycle is its disclosure of the seer's powerlessness to see beyond a certain point, in the form of an open book of questions. And this in turn brings into view another threshold. From the naming of truth, albeit the truth of the reader's blindness, reading, in a key modulation, turns into a venture that makes more tenuous yet its links to a philosophical or cognitive quest. It becomes part of an activity discerned by the hero in all domains of life, most visibly in the creations of the cycle's artists and artisans, namely invention, which works with the tangible realities at hand, to revise them, "translate" them, to bring forth a new design.

As the cycle's tale of the book to come moves backwards to that book's pre-texts as "deciphered" by Marcel Proust, and forwards toward the book's uncertain prospects in a future that lies beyond the novel's end, the narrator, its central, allegorical reader, becomes a figure in a chain of readers. Preceded by his progenitor, he is slated in the end to pass on his task to a new reader in and of a world which will already once again demand, in his words, "to be totally redrawn;"[3] for, even as it appears doomed, it holds the secret of renewal.

I.

Pre-Texts

Gerda R. Blumenthal

1. Reading: Reality and Metaphor

Long before the Proustian narrator dreams of becoming a writer, and almost a whole lifetime before the hero of *A la recherche* grasps the link between writing his novel and reading the "inner book" of his life, he is an insatiable reader of real books. Throughout Proust's *oeuvre*—from the early *Pastiches*, through the translations, essays and articles of his Ruskin and post-Ruskin period, through *Jean Santeuil, Contre Sainte-Beuve* and, finally, *A la recherche*—the sheer force of presence of the narrator's precursors, as Margaret Mein has called them,[1] is matched only by his own astounding power of assimilation. The foremost of these precursors range from his seventeenth century masters Racine and the *moralistes*, Pascal, La Rochefoucauld and La Bruyère, to the nineteenth century masters of fiction, its poets of memory, Chateaubriand, Nerval and Baudelaire, and of course, Ruskin, apostle of the beauty of Gothic cathedrals and the stones of Venice. In the course of the slow emergence of *A la recherche* out of its own Proustian pre-texts, the narrative voice of a voracious reader first mimicks and echoes, then gradually assimilates his master's voices until, even as his reader continues to recognize with delight the most familiar resonances—a passage of "pure Racine" here, of "pure Saint-Simon" there—this voice becomes one of the most compelling in all fiction.

In turn, books "magnetize" the world for the hero of *A la recherche*. They first lead him out of himself into ever-expanding worlds of the non-self which his imagination hungrily absorbs and assimilates, then slowly to an increasingly penetrating deciphering both of his inner book and of the complex nature of a book's truth-telling power, and ultimately to the threshold of composing his own novel. *La Recherche* could serve admirably to demonstrate the point that books are born of other books.[2] However, Proust's tale of the book to come is a far less literary adventure story than such a demonstration might imply. The role of books in the future writer's life is invariably and at first overwhelmingly a *contextual* one. The books he reads may speak to his deepest dreams and aspirations, but they are above all inseparably linked to the specific moments and settings of the act of reading, which thus become an integral part of their meaning for him.

From the time of his childhood, when his mother read *François le Champi* to him one night, to the years when the mature narrator of *Contre Sainte-Beuve* shows his mother the power and spiritual depth of Baudelaire's vision in *Les Fleurs du Mal*, especially in the condemned poems which are morally repellent to her, or the victory of Gérard's creative will over hallucination in *Sylvie*; or, again, when the hero explains to Albertine, in *La Prisonnière*, the stark new truths about the human heart's ambivalence which Dostoevsky's novels first laid bare, the hero's relationship to books differs, as we shall see, from that of other readers in *La Recherche*. In its depth and originality it is as different from his grandmother's and mother's cult of their marquise, Mme de Sévigné, as from M. de Charlus' cult of Balzac, the melancholy bookishness of Legrandin or the "Beuvian" judgments of Mme de Villeparisis.

In *La Recherche*, but even more so in the earlier texts, some of Proust's most amusing and devastating satires are aimed at a variegated collection of readers *manqués*. In "Le Balzac de M. de Guermantes,"[3] the Count de Guermantes has found his *raison d'être* in becoming a Balzac "expert," and in enjoying the daily ritual of hiding from his guests in his upstairs library with "his" Balzac: "Mme de Guermantes would explain to persons who didn't know: 'My husband, you know, when you get him on Balzac, it's like the stereoscope; he'll tell you where every picture comes from, the country it represents; I don't know how he can remember it all...'" (269). In the same chapter, Mme de Villeparisis makes her first appearance as the "intelligent reader," whose positivist, cultural-biographical approach to books is clearly a parody of Sainte-Beuve's. She firmly judges a work by what she knows of its author's life—and since almost all the writers discussed in her salon frequented her father's house when she was young, she has "known" them all—and by the author's knowledge of real life. On both counts she dismisses the author of *La Comédie humaine* with scorn: he was, as everyone who knew him would confirm, a vulgar man who, moreover, saw only the negative side of things; besides, he was not even received in the high society he presumed to write about. Alongside those two, Proust places the young Marquise de Cardaillec, who exemplifies the idolatrous imitator. In the illusion that her dreary existence will gain luster by being framed in a famous fictional décor, she turns the house which her husband has inherited in Alençon into a kind of Balzac museum, replete with details out of the lives of Mlle Cormon and Mme de Bargeton. All the characters in this gallery of *literati* have in common a basic misunderstanding of reading, which, whatever particular form it may take, is compounded of snobbery, shallowness and barrenness of imagination.

These satirical portrayals take on a more tragic dimension in *La Recherche*, where they are brought to bear on characters endowed with real creative gifts. The hero clearly discerns a warning to himself in the aborted lives of Swann and M. de Charlus, who have both misspent their idealism, imagination and will by turning the works they love into cult objects and compensations for a disillusioning existence. Nothing can grow out of their sterile readings which have increasingly become for both exercises in nostalgia if not self-deception. There is something poignant but also perversely literary in M. de Charlus' finding a momentary reprieve from his unhappy love for Morel in seeing Albertine dressed in gray, because, as he tells her, it is the gray worn by Mme de Cadignan for her first meeting with d'Arthez. In a similar vein, Swann draws on the power of Botticelli and Vinteuil to endow Odette with a beauty that his listless imagination, no longer able to magnetize objects, is unable to discern in her without help. Anxious only to appropriate the sonata's "little phrase" for himself and Odette as a "national anthem" and pledge of their love, Swann is unwilling to heed the little phrase's secret, its song of love's vanity: "In its airy grace there was the sense of something over and done with, like the mood of philosophic detachment which follows an outburst of vain regret. But all that mattered little to him; he contemplated the little phrase less in its own light—in what it might express to a musician who knew nothing of the existence of him and Odette when he had composed it, and to all those who would hear it in centuries to come—than as a pledge, a token of his love. . ." (1:238; 1:218).

Well above these sterile misreaders who seek refuge and justification in art, Proust places the fervent idealists whose favorite book serves them as a sacred text in a different way. The hero's mother and grandmother are without doubt the purest, most ardent and selfless characters in *La Recherche*, but their imagination, alas, lags behind their moral virtues and greatness of heart. They are sentimental readers for whom the letters of Mme de Sévigné represent the ultimate embodiment of maternal love, civilized human relationships, refinement of mind and turn of phrase. Emulating her, quoting her, applying her pithy comments to situations in their own lives is an inexhaustible source of joy to them. Yet all this constant reading and quoting by heart of the beloved text does not lead them a step beyond the text in their own perception of reality. They remain disciples. Reading, Proust had warned his own reader years earlier in "Sur la lecture," can only incite the imagination to do its work; it cannot do that work for it. When in that essay he fought off the grip of Ruskin's estheticism on his own imagination by attacking the master's exalted praise of reading in "Kings' Treasuries," he took pains to point out that reading can easily turn into an act of idolatry. When reading is extolled, as Ruskin extolled it in that lecture of 1864, as an act of spiritual communion in which the truth is passed on from master to disciple, and glorified as one of the highest achievements of the spirit, it becomes a threat to the creative will: "To make a discipline of it is to give too great a role to what is but an incitement. Reading is at the threshold of spiritual life; it can introduce us to it; it does not constitute it."[4]

The hero of *A la recherche* is especially vulnerable to the danger of idolatry. He is a passionate quester after an ideal world of truth, morbidly impressionable, and all too ready to receive the truth from his idols rather than make the effort to decipher it by himself. Only an incorruptible lucidity and fidelity to his own feelings and impressions, strengthened by the lessons his masters have taught him, will lead him to realize that no book written by another can put him in possession of the truth he is pursuing. A charmingly simple version of this lesson is given to the hero's precursor, Jean Santeuil, by Jean's teacher, M. Beulier.

A few days before New Year, Jean has brought his teacher a small bust as a New Year present. When M. Beulier comes to his house for a lesson on New Year's eve, he in turn brings his pupil a gift. " 'I too am bringing you a present.' It was a book by Joubert. For two hours, M. Beulier read it with Jean; when they had finished . . ., at the moment when Jean, looking at the book, said: 'No present has given me more pleasure,' M. Beulier took the book, put it in his briefcase and never brought it back. Having given Jean all of its meaning, its soul, its moral support, he had given him all of it. Therein lay the priceless and pure gift."[5]

M. Beulier's gift teaches Jean that books are beacons and mediators, not personal possessions or ultimate truths to live by. Throughout the long seeding period of the hero's own book that lasts throughout *A la recherche*, the reading of books, in its successive metamorphoses, becomes a paradigm of the complex process of registering and deciphering, transcribing and composing reality, which the act of writing alone will consummate. For in its own way, the visible text in the bound volume he holds in his hand is no less a palimpsest than the inner book of impressions. What it tells on the surface may captivate a reader like M. de Guermantes, especially if, like *La Comédie humaine*, it guilefully presents itself as an encyclopedia of French life. But this surface is a screen which intimates but also hides a deeper truth, not of fact, but of vision. Significantly, even though the vast majority of characters in *La Recherche* are assiduous readers, the budding writer alone, aided by his artist-mentors, becomes a real reader in the Proustian sense who, in the course of his life, will find his way into the most hidden substrata of a text and whose imagination is able to assimilate and will ultimately seek to recompose what it has found there for its own creative purposes.

In its initial, largely pre-conscious phase, reading in the hero's life is more than anything else a child's passionate dreaming in response to a tale's mystery, its incomprehensible but all the more glorious intimation of "another" world which lies beyond the familiar and not so interesting world of his every-day life. The hero is still quite small when his mother first reads to him *François le Champi* in those nocturnal hours that wreak havoc with his normal schedule. This suspension of the routine timetable, his mother's presence which breaks the most sacred taboo and exceeds his most reckless hopes of only moments before, the book's strange, melodious title and "vivid, ruddy, charming colour," above all, the mother's voice as she reads, combine to arouse in him a keen excitement and sense of anticipation. The very inaccessibility of the story's meaning to his childish mind, further compounded by his mother's skipping over all the love scenes, opens up large gaps in the story for dreaming as his mind alternately strains to understand what he hears and wanders off into its own revery. It also allows the contextual elements of the reading—his complex feelings of fascination, guilt and delight and the multiple sense impressions engendered by the setting in which the reading takes place—to come into full play.

The harvest of these childhood readings then, in which the particular text is almost unimportant and might easily have been another, is less a specific truth gleaned from a specific book which his mind can clearly discern, than a total and unique configuration of dreams, feelings and sense impressions which the inner book of his self registers avidly. Any distinction between "high" and "low" signs in this complex registering process would be artificial, as the text makes clear, since it would break up into separate levels an experience characterized, on the contrary, by a single, total upsurge of the reader's whole being, grounded in his faith in and hunger for "another," ideal world of truth.

> Upon the sort of screen dappled with different states and impressions which my consciousness would simultaneously unfold while I was reading, and which ranged from the most deeply hidden aspirations of my heart to the wholly external view of the horizon spread out before my eyes..., what was my primary, my innermost impulse, the lever whose incessant movements controlled everything else, was my belief in the philosophical richness and beauty of the book I was reading, and my desire to appropriate them to myself, whatever the book might be. (1:90; 1:84)

The figure through which the middle-aged narrator evokes those childhood hours of reading and the twofold dream they engender of love and of journeys, is that of a surging fountain. In reconciling the reader's physical immobility with the outward thrust of his imagination eager to take possession of the world evoked by the book, the figure captures the truth of reading as a veritable marriage feast between knowledge and desire and between self and world, in which all separateness is overcome. In the reader's obliviousness to the striking of the hour, the "moments" embodied in those dreams and which he will later be reduced to recapturing separately, sequentially, are experienced as part of a total, indivisible fullness of being: "I isolate (them) artificially today, explains the narrator, as though I were cutting sections of different heights in a jet of water, iridescent but seemingly without flow or motion... in a single, undeviating, irresistible outpouring of all the forces of my life."[6] Moreover, he recognizes, any qualitative distinction between higher and lower levels in the young reader's responses to his book is misleading in another way. For paradoxically, if the higher imprints are those made on the mind by the book's intellectually accessible content, and the lower ones, those multiple contextual impressions that remain inaccessible to the mind by dint of their vagueness or their moral or intellectual insignificance, the latter are far more vital and abiding. They will remain the faithful custodians of a specific and therefore irreplaceable moment of the reader's life, out of which his memory and imagination will one day compose a timeless moment in a new book of hours.

Towards the end of *Le Temps retrouvé*, when the hero's hopes for the future are all but dead and George Sand's fiction has lost whatever charm it may once have had for him, the sight of *François le Champi* on a shelf of the Prince de Guermantes' library stirs him as deeply as the uneven flagstones in the Guermantes courtyard, the starched napkin or the clinking sound of the spoon. This inner upheaval has less than ever to do with George Sand's actual text, the sentimental tale that many years back had set him dreaming. It is as part of his own inner book now, and with the irresistible vigor of his miraculously resurrected childhood faith, that the book demands to be deciphered:

> My first reaction had been to ask myself, angrily, who this stranger was who was coming to trouble me. The stranger was none other than myself, the child I had been at that time, brought to life within me by the book which, knowing nothing of me except this child, had instantly summoned him to its presence, wanting to be seen only by his eyes, to be loved only by his heart, to speak only to him... Admittedly the "pen" of George Sand... no longer seemed to me, as for so long it had seemed to my mother before she had gradually come to model her literary tastes upon mine, in the least a magic pen. But it was a pen which, unintentionally, like a schoolboy amusing himself with a real pen, I had charged with electricity, and now a thousand trifling details of Combray which for years had not entered my mind came lightly and spontaneously leaping, in follow-my-leader fashion, to suspend themselves from the magnetized nib in an interminable and trembling chain of memories. (3:919; 3:884)

Thus, in its earliest stage, the Proustian act of reading is one of the most richly constitutive of the hero's inner book or pre-text of the book to come. Like his rapt contemplation before the white and pink hawthorns of Tansonville, it has the power to abolish his sense of time as it inscribes in him indelibly a concrete, unique moment of his childhood.

This vital link between text and existential context will remain characteristic of the hero's reading life, even when he learns to decipher the books he reads more lucidly. The initial dichotomy in his mind between the "otherworldliness" of books and the realities of the here and now gives way to an increasingly dynamic interaction between the two. Slowly, as he grows older and begins to heed the silent appeals addressed to him everywhere by things around him and by the fictional heroes whose adventures he now follows with feverish attention, the mysterious "other" world to which his whole being aspires, reveals itself to be not "out of this world," but rather a "translation" or transfiguration of the real one. The books he reads are no longer a vague music that allows his dreams to soar. He now turns to them with an impatient need to learn the secret meaning behind real gestures, faces, words and objects, which direct experience keeps promising to reveal but in reality conceals from him; for

> a "real" person, profoundly as we may sympathize with him, is in a great measure perceptible only through our senses, that is to say, remains opaque, presents a dead weight which our sensibilities have not the strength to lift . . . . The novelist's happy discovery was to think of substituting for those opaque sections immaterial sections, things, that is, which one's soul can assimilate. After which it matters not that the actions, the feelings of this new order of creatures appears to us in the guise of truth, since we have made them our own, since it is in ourselves that they are happening, that they are holding in thrall, as we feverishly turn over the pages of the book, our quickened breath and staring eyes. And once the novelist has brought us to this state, in which, as in all purely mental states, every emotion is multiplied ten-fold, into which his book comes to disturb us as might a dream, but a dream more lucid and more abiding than those which come to us in sleep, why then, for the space of an hour he sets free within us all the joys and sorrows in the world, a few of which only we should have to spend years of our actual life in getting to know, and the most intense of which would never be revealed to us because the slow course of their development prevents us from perceiving them. It is the same in life; the heart changes, and it is our worst sorrow; but we know it only through reading, through our imagination . . . . (1:91-92; 1:85)

In the silent communion between his own faith and the storyteller's art which, by means of fictional illusion, has created a perfect simulacrum of the sought-after truth, a novel's landscape, no matter how contingent its original choice by the writer may have been, presents itself to the reader as "a true part of Nature herself, worthy of being studied and probed." Books now magnetize the real world of his every-day life. Far from stilling his appetite, the illusions of fiction make him return to reality with a more impassioned, hungry alertness. First of all, he discovers to his chagrin that books are always incomplete. They suddenly come to a stop, like Scheherazade's tale at dawn, leaving him in cruel uncertainty about the future of the hero whose fate he has made his own. His perplexed imagination has to take over where they have left off. But even the truths they do tell him and which enchant him merely enhance his eagerness to uncover by himself and take possession of the treasures which he now feels await him everywhere.

Both literally and metaphorically, reading makes him hungry. Repeatedly, both in *Jean Santeuil* and *A la recherche*, the young hero's gluttonous feasts of reading precede culinary feasts that are being prepared within range of his nostrils by the family's "Michelangelo of the kitchen" while he is lost in his book. Several hours of voracious reading become preludes to joyous hours spent at table devouring Ernestine-Françoise's succulent chickens, roastbeefs, asparagus, chocolate creams, or his favorite dessert, strawberries crushed in cream cheese. The same basic appetite leads him from the silent, "extra-temporal" hours of reading to the gregarious, sensuous, tyrannically clock-bound Proustian meals: to ingest and assimilate more and more of life's riches and, unbeknownst to himself, feed the inner book he carries within him. As the cook's art, abetted by the sacred fires of her "forge," transforms an obstreperous chicken in the yard, seeking escape from her knife, into a rich, delicious fare for his stomach and senses, so the story which he reads in his aunt's quiet, sunlit backyard converts the immediate and therefore impenetrable realities of life into a dematerialized, fully assimilable food for his imagination. In both instances, the stories read and the meals eaten mediate between him and the world of raw, unmediated reality, pre-deciphering and processing that world in a way that demands of him nothing more than an eager receptivity.

In time, both books and real life begin to demand more. The novels of Bergotte open up a new and crucial dimension of truth, which lies as far beyond the vagueness of his other-worldly childhood dreams as it does beyond the wholly accessible worldly truths of traditional fiction and roast chicken. What instantly captivates the adolescent hero in Bergotte's texts of which Bloch has spoken with such admiration is nothing like the providential design of an adventure story in which all is clear and explicit. The "doux chantre"'s voice is a narrative voice unlike any he has ever heard before and which in its strangeness defies his understanding. Though he feels transported by the truth of Bergotte's novels, he is unable to translate this truth into ideas. It is like the "song of a harp" arising from an "unknown world." Not yet able to understand that the truth of Bergotte's novels *is* that unique voice which is opening up a whole new register of chords in his sensibility, he tries in vain to discover Bergotte's opinions about everything, from Gothic cathedrals to la Berma's acting. Yet, while his mind, hungry for clear ideas, is ostensibly being starved by the texts' elusiveness, it is being harnessed surreptitiously to his imagination's effort to decipher their hidden poetic design. At first he can discern nothing. Then gradually, as he becomes more familiar with those novels, the fog clears and a pattern becomes visible:

> For the first few days, like a tune with which one will soon be infatuated but which one has not yet 'got hold' of, the things I was to love so passionately in Bergotte's style did not immediately strike me. I could not, it is true, lay down the novel of his which I was reading, but I fancied that I was interested in the subject alone, as in the first dawn of love when we go every day to meet a woman at some party or entertainment which we think is in itself the attraction. Then I observed the rare, almost archaic expressions he liked to employ at certain points, in which a hidden stream of harmony, an inner prelude would heighten his style.... One of these passages of Bergotte, the third or fourth which I had detached from the rest, filled me with a joy to which the meager joy I had tasted in the first passage bore no comparison, a joy that I felt I was experiencing in a deeper, vaster, more integral part of myself, from which all obstacles and partitions seemed to have been swept away.... I now had the impression of being confronted not by a particular passage in one of Bergotte's works, tracing a purely bi-dimensional figure upon the surface of my mind, but rather by the 'ideal passage' of Bergotte, common to every one of his books, to which all the earlier, similar passages, now becoming merged in it, had added a kind of density and volume by which my own understanding seemed to be enlarged. (1:101-102; 1:93-94)

The text slowly reveals itself to him as a palimpsest which leads the reader from its gleaming, undulating surface through the intermediate layers of its more or less intellectually accessible subject matter and ideas to the deepest truths of the writer's inner world. Each of us, the hero muses, carries his own world within him—a world unique and different from every other—, but such a text alone has the power to communicate it to others.

He discovers that the paradoxical fascination of a great text lies in its demand for an intellectual deciphering as much as in its mystery which defies and transcends elucidation. Many hundreds of pages after his discovery of Bergotte, we find him once again engaged in seeking to decipher unfamiliar compositions which this time Albertine is playing for him on the pianola: "I liked to fix my thoughts only upon what was still obscure to me and to be able, in the course of these successive renderings, thanks to the increasing but, alas, distorting and alien light of my intellect, to link to one another the fragmentary and interrupted lines of the structure which at first had been almost hidden in mist" (3:378-379; 3:371-372). Each success scored by his analytical mind in its "nefarious" task of reducing the ineffable appeal of a text or composition to a definable truth, yields him the gain of a truth, satisfying the mind's need for general laws—physical, psychological or compositional—but at the price of a piece of music. No sooner have the hero's increasingly formidable powers of analysis uncovered a text's secret design, than the text's spell is broken and his interest propelled on to a new, still unfathomed text. In sharp contrast to the reading habits of most other characters in *A la recherche*, the hero's reading life moves through a succession of books, each of which opens up a particular truth or vision vital to him which he deciphers and makes his own, but which does not, with the exception of a few great texts, remain for long in the foreground of his consciousness.

Significantly, the works whose power remains inexhaustible, which continue to feed the deepest needs of his being from the beginning to the end of *A la recherche*, are not literary compositions but musical ones. It is not in a book but in the compositions of Vinteuil that he discovers that ineffable translucency of fully transfigured, "recomposed" human emotions, which constitutes both the highest truth for him and the most resistant to cognitive decipherings, and which thus becomes an unequalled paradigm for his own book to come:

> ... this music seemed to me to be something truer than all known books. At moments I thought that this was due to the fact that what we feel in life not being felt in the form of ideas, its literary, that is to say intellectual expression describes it, explains it, analyzes it, but does not recompose it as does music, in which the sounds seem to follow the very movement of our being, to reproduce that extreme inner point of our

sensations which is the part that gives us that peculiar exhilaration which we experience from time to time and which, when we say: "What a fine day! What glorious sunshine!" we do not in the least communicate to others....
Thus nothing resembled more closely than some such phrase of Vinteuil the peculiar pleasure which I had felt at certain moments of my life, when gazing, for instance, at the steeples of Martinville, or at certain trees along a road near Balbec, or, more simply, at the beginning of this book, when I tasted a certain cup of tea. (3:381; 3:374)

Unlike Swann who blindly appropriated the "little phrase" to feed an illusion, the lover's illusion of a communion between himself and the beloved, which Vinteuil's sonata evokes on the contrary *as* an illusion in the two instruments' plaintive dialogue, the hero discerns in the composer's septet a paradigm for the kind of truth which his book will in turn have to decipher, "transcribe" and compose. It will have to reach beyond the purely confessional elements of personal recollection, but also beyond those general truths about life which can be defined analytically and named aphoristically. And it will have to do so not by denying or eschewing either of these orders of truth, but by assuming them fully and transcending them through its power of song. Vinteuil's music answers no questions, but by transporting him to the depth of his own being through the "divine round" of its figures, it sets him free and produces in him that special rapture, "more real, more fecund" than any other, which transforms even his suffering and his unanswered questions into sources of hope and creative energy.

On that level, reading does indeed take a foremost place in *A la recherche* among the privileged moments which yield an intimation of another, "extra-temporal" world. Unlike the evanescent, fugitive eternities of memory and poetic sensations, books have the power to capture this intimation for the reader in figural constellations which endure. But because books too are powerless to create that other world in an ontological sense, they make palpable even in their fullness the distance that is always yet to be bridged. Hence their role in the cycle as pre-texts of a book forever still to come.

2. Threshold Creations

In the Proustian cycle's twofold movement, all at once retrospective and prospective, in which an ostensibly completed story is recaptured while a new book is secretly striving to emerge, the budding writer's attention is continually drawn back—and in a deeper sense forward—from such finished masterpieces as Bergotte's novels, Vinteuil's septet or Vermeer's "View of Delft," to works which either remain intrinsically embedded in life or which have about them something of the incompleteness of sketches. Like many actual writers or painters before him, Delacroix for example, who often preferred a fellow artist's sketches to his finished compositions,[1] the budding writer who is instinctively assembling the pre-texts of his book and reflecting on his craft, responds with special keenness to works which are still "half-sheathed" in the specific place or occasion of their origin. Not yet fully emancipated, these works highlight for him that all-important threshold moment in the creative process in which the fortuitously joined elements of a given reality can be seen calling forth a formal design which will "translate" them into meaning.

In his tribute to Ruskin, "Journées de Pèlerinage," written in 1900, the young Proust first explained this special predilection which was to lose none of its strength in later years, and which sheds light on one of the most persistent impulses at work in the Proustian text, namely the urge to disassemble finished formal designs, including its own, by uncovering their pre-texts, and thus to restore to visibility the vital interaction between the individual and constantly shifting realities of life and artistic forms which the sharp dividing line drawn between them by a Symbolist poetic has tended to obscure. Two small reproductions on his desk, one of the Joconda, the other of the Gilded Virgin of the south portal of the Cathedral of Amiens, lead him to reflect on the preference, wholly unjustified from a purely esthetic viewpoint, which he feels for the latter. The Joconda is a "homeless" masterpiece, autonomous, wholly emancipated from the original context of the place, time and personal experience that brought her forth. She is the same wherever she may be. In contrast to her, the Amiens Virgin is an Amiénoise, inseparable from her particular spot on the portal which has remained her medieval home. But because of that clearly visible link, she has far more to say to a budding writer (here Proust himself) heeding the demands of a book still deeply buried in his own inner book of experience, and who is seeking to understand the relationship between the book to be written and the uniquely personal context of his life. A true threshold creation whose life is as much the product of her medieval sculptor as it is a living, changing part of the place to which she belongs, she makes visible to him the specific context out of which are born even the most universal masterpieces. More than that, she enriches his inner "sketchbook" by resurrecting for him one of the most exalted moments of his personal past, his pilgrimage to Amiens, in which a particular moment of medieval history, embodied in a particular town and its square, became linked with his special love for the man who for years was his spiritual mentor, John Ruskin.

> I feel that I was wrong in calling her a work of art: a statue which thus forms forever part of a particular place on earth, that is to say of something which bears a name like a person, which is an individual the exact like of whom one could never find on the face of the continents, of which the station master, in calling out its name at the place to which one has had no choice but to come in order to find it, seems without knowing it to tell us: "Love that which you shall never see again," such a statue has perhaps something less universal about it than a work of art; but it holds us by a stronger bond than the work of art itself, one of those bonds as create, to keep their hold on us, persons and countries. The Joconda is Da Vinci's Joconda. What does her birthplace matter to us, or even that she has become French by naturalization? She is something like an admirable "citizen of the world" .... One cannot say the same of her smiling and sculpted sister (who, needless to say, is far inferior to her). The Gilded Virgin ... is truly an Amiénoise. She is not a work of art. She is a lovely friend whom we must leave behind on the melancholy provincial square whence no one has succeeded in taking her away, and where she will continue to receive in her face the wind and sun of Amiens, to let the small sparrows settle, with a sure decorative instinct, in the hollow of her outstretched hand or pick the stone stamen of the ancient hawthorns which for so many centuries have been her youthful adornment. In my room, a photograph of the Joconda retains only the beauty of a masterpiece. Near it, the photograph of the Gilded Virgin takes on the wistfulness of a memory. (*Pastiches et mélanges*, 84-85)

Defying his quest for universal laws and essences, she is a powerful reminder to the writer that his book, if it is to achieve a measure of universality, must be a "translation" or transfiguration of the distinctive places and persons that have embodied life's successive seasons. Indeed, she herself is a living testimony to the inseparability of persons and places which will become a hallmark of the Proustian hero's experience and of the Proustian text. Persons and places become virtually interchangeable in *A la recherche*, as Georges Poulet has shown,[2] to the point where the hero is not sure whether he loves Albertine because he has seen her rise like a sea goddess out of the ocean at Balbec, or whether Balbec remains precious to him because he first encountered Albertine on its beach. The same intimate link binds together Combray and his family, the Champs-Elysées and Gilberte, the Bois de Boulogne and Odette or, in *Contre Sainte-Beuve*, Guermantes and its lords. Throughout the texts, places are consistently endowed with a more distinct personality than characters. In their irreducible specificity they quite literally constitute the ground out of which not only the hero's book, but all the diverse artistic designs that he encounters in the course of his apprenticeship, can be seen burgeoning. Not invented, not dreamed up, but concrete and verifiable—by such things as train schedules which enthrall him—they have the power to authenticate a composition's truth for him, to guarantee that no matter how high the latter may soar metaphorically, it remains linked to and continues to hold discourse with life.

It is no wonder then that churches play a special role in virtually all of the major texts. Beyond the indisputable role which Ruskin played in "magnetizing" for the young Proust the Gothic cathedrals of France and northern Italy, the conjunction they embody of a spiritual and artistic truth and an abiding rootedness and participation in daily life, makes them veritable grammars of composition for the hero, both in *Jean Santeuil* and *A la recherche*. Like the Gilded Virgin, the church of Combray is not strictly speaking a work of art, but it is one of the cycle's great mediators between time and place and a timeless universality. For all its power to universalize the particular cycle of hours and seasons of Combray through its liturgy, the ringing of its bells which summon the faithful and spread the good news across the countryside, and in its stones, statuary, stained glass and tapestries, Saint-Hilaire remains the naturalized citizen of Combray, whose people it serves, whose pigeons find shelter in its abutments, and whose passing seasons age it as they age the village's human inhabitants, flora and fauna. "For human creations, by dint of being fixed in a place in nature, end up by becoming part of it, to the point where the latter attracts us by a kind of half human personality, and they by a kind of local charm.... It seems as if their artistic beauty had taken roots and little by little, like the place to which it is attached, become something unique and which does not depend on man, something that nothing can bring to us if we do not go back there" (*Jean Santeuil*, 366).

Half-way between the fully emancipated masterpieces and the ephemeral arts of life, these naturalized works in stone interact so vigorously with the immediate life surrounding them that, however ancient they may be in years, they retain an abiding freshness. But they have something else to teach the hero who until the very end of the cycle asserts that writing his book will be a "reading" of universal laws. Even a modest country church like Saint-Hilaire, for all its conformity to the general laws of Gothic architecture, has an individual style of its own that makes it unlike any other church. Whether it is in the *leitmotiv* of the Guermantes or the noble simplicity of its steeple, it bears the distinct mark of the inventiveness and originality of its builders, sculptors and weavers. And not only is there no conflict between its distinctive character and the fidelity with which it translates the Scriptures for the faithful into a Bible of stones and stained glass and obeys liturgical and architectural canons but, on the contrary, it is able to offer a true "reading" only because it is able to weave that truth out of the materials provided it by the present. However persistently *A la recherche* disguises its own inventiveness, it takes great care to place signals all along its hero's path to lead him to understand that a book, like any other composition, is far from being a simple transcription of a given, pre-existing truth. It is an augural event through which all that has been is transformed, takes on a new face and a new meaning. This originality marks not only the masterpieces in which, needless to say, it is most powerful, but it can already be discerned in the myriad threshold creations which are scattered throughout *Jean Santeuil* and *A la recherche*. Moreover, it is in these works which are still visibly bound to their pre-texts that a style's emergence and its power to transform the given can be seen most clearly.

In a short meditation on Claude Monet's garden at Giverny, written in 1907, Proust dreams of going to Giverny to see the garden that served the painter as a model for some of his greatest works. In his mind he retraces the three successive stages that marked the birth of those paintings. The first, a luxuriant flower garden, bespeaks nature's own creative abundance; in the second, the natural garden is transformed through the painter's careful planting into a "painterly" garden of tones and colors; finally, the painterly garden is "translated" into the master's paintings. Significantly, the essay's emphasis is on the second, threshold stage, in which the first, "living" sketch is still visible just before the painter's design asserts its full autonomy:

> ... if ... I can one day see Claude Monet's garden, I am sure I shall see, in a garden of tones and colors even more than of flowers, a garden which must be less the former florist-garden than, if I can put it that way, a colorist-garden of flowers arranged in a composition which is not quite nature's, since they were planted in such a way as to let only those flowers bloom at the same time whose shades would harmonize and blend as far as the eye could see in an expanse of blue and rose, and which the powerfully evident intention of the painter has abstracted in some sort from all that is not color. They are flowers of earth and also flowers of water, those delicate water-lilies which the master depicted on sublime canvases, of which the garden (already a true artistic transposition rather than a mere model for a painting, already a painting composed in nature which comes to light under the eye of a great painter) is as it were the first and living sketch, or at least the ready and exquisite palette on which the harmonious tones are prepared.
> (*Essais et articles*, 539-540)

In contrast to a Swann or any of the idolaters who people *A la recherche*, for whom Monet's garden would be hallowed ground because the master immortalized it in his "Water-Lilies," the budding writer attributed to it no such special status. He knew that that particular garden was for the painter simply part of what Delacroix called the "dictionary" with which nature provides the artist and in which he finds what he needs for his own creative purposes.[3] The passage sheds a great deal of light on the unexpected way in which Proust's own and his hero's fascination with a work's pre-texts ultimately converges with the "wrongheaded" quest of a Sainte-Beuve. The critic's method of seeking the connection between a writer's life and his works, between a given reality and its artistic transformation followed the wrong order, but the connection itself is as strongly sought out in the

Proustian texts as it is in Sainte-Beuve's essays. There is hardly a composition in *A la recherche*, literary or other, not to speak of the book to come, which the hero does not end up tracing back, however incompletely and seemingly by happenstance, to an early sketch, to marvel both at the utter unpredictability of that sketch's metamorphosis into the finished work and its power, retrospectively, to illuminate it. "Certain comparisons which are false if we start from them as premises may well be true if we arrive at them as conclusions," he notes in *Le Temps retrouvé*. Nothing in "Miss Sacripant," Elstir's early water-color sketch of the not at all beautiful, drawn-looking young actress in the provocative costume could have foretold either the radiant beauty of the mature Mme Swann, goddess in the Elysean Garden of Woman, or the manner of the painter's later canvases; but in retrospect it is a revelation. In turn, nothing on his own part, the narrator muses, would have been more sterile than a conscious ambition from the start to turn his life into a book and, in imitation of the painters, to keep a sketchbook or diary in which he would note down his impressions day by day. Indeed, the Proustian book is the diametrical opposite of a journal or diary, since a diary's entries, in producing the closest possible coincidence between immediate impressions and their transcription, suppress the very distance between the two that frees the imagination to do its composing. Only the book itself will reveal to its writer that he has kept a diary or sketchbook all along:

> The man of letters envies the painter, he would like to take notes and make sketches, but it would be disastrous for him to do so. Yet when he writes, there is not a single gesture of his characters, not a trick of behavior, not a tone of voice which has not been supplied to his inspiration by his memory; beneath the name of every character of his invention he can put sixty names of characters that he has seen, one of whom has posed for the grimace, another for the monocle, another for their fits of temper . . ., etc. And in the end the writer realizes that if his dream of being a sort of painter was not in a conscious and intentional manner capable of fulfilment, it has nevertheless been fulfilled and that he too, for his work as a writer, has unconsciously made use of a sketchbook. (3:936-937; 3:899-890)

Among the most illuminating designs inscribed by *A la recherche* in its hero's inner sketchbook are the ephemeral compositions of a host of "natural" precursors, ranging from nature herself to some of the otherwise least interesting characters to cross the hero's path. Their creations are modest indeed. They do not outlast the hour or season of their emergence and triumph. They are not metaphors of universal human truths whose depth and magnitude can resist time and changing fashions and abide, if not eternally, at least for generations. But to the budding writer they are a source of special excitement because they are born of and, in turn, work their miracles on the most ordinary moments of his daily life. Not only do they give magic to those hours, but they too offer special insight into the process of "reading" and "translating" reality.

Nature, the hero realizes in *Le Temps retrouvé*, was the first to teach him the art of creating metaphors out of pure metonymy. An unconscious composer of synesthesia, continually interweaving light, sounds, smells and sight, she showed him how to empower a single element of a moment filled to overflowing with feeling and sensations to carry the message of every other element and, thus, of the total moment: "Had not nature herself - if one considered the matter from this point of view - placed me on the path of art, was she not herself a beginning of art, she who, often, had allowed me to become aware of the beauty of one thing only in another thing, of the beauty, for instance, of noon at Combray in the sound of its bells, of that of mornings at Doncières in the hiccups of our central heating? The link may be uninteresting, the object trivial, the style bad, but unless this process has taken place, the description is worthless" (3:925; 3:889-890).

In defiance of the cycle's overt assertions which, ironically, echo the bourgeois'—a Mme Verdurin's—esthetic creed, this passage unmasks as false any radical dichotomy between art and life in which the former is made to stand for the full presence, and the latter the total absence of a meaningful, life-enhancing principle of coherence. Not only does the hero discern figurative designs of elemental force if rudimentary form in nature herself, but he bestows some of his highest, most exuberant tributes to what, in contrast to the "arts of nothingness" practiced by the "patronne" and her more refined counterparts in the Faubourg Saint-Germain, could be called the arts of life, and which conform perfectly to the laws of authentic creation.

These arts of life are clearly more artisan than artistic in character, but this rigid line of demarcation too the cycle reveals to be misleading. Underneath the playfulness with which both *Jean Santeuil* and *A la recherche* exaggerate and multiply the analogies between a Félicie or Françoise and Michelangelo, a deliberate design is at work to take the book to come out of the falsely circumscribed, closed domain called "art," and to retrace it, in the most anti-Symbolist, most classical fashion possible, to its pretexts in life. Like the ancient Greeks who did not create works of art to be set apart from the vases, vessels and other utensils they made for their daily use, or Françoise's medieval artisan ancestors of Saint-André-des-Champs who did not view their anonymous labors in building and sculpting their church as creating a work of art, so Proust's tale of the book, for all its contrary assertions, evokes a continuous process of reshaping the world in which artists and artisans can be seen engaged in wholly analogous pursuits. In his modest sphere, the artisan composes his work with the immediate, natural gifts of a season, climate, vegetable garden, or near-by butcher shop or grocery. The occasion that demands his supreme effort may be nothing more momentous than having M. de Norpois to dinner. On the complex and mysterious level of the painter's art, the given elements are the majestic water, land and ships of the Port of Carquethuit; the occasion is the painter's inner need to break down the false and congealed dividing line between land and water which pictorial convention has perpetuated, and to make visible their true interpenetration. But both cook and painter are engaged in fundamentally the same endeavor; namely, starting with the given, to decompose, then to recompose it into a new, more truly life-sustaining form.

In *Jean Santeuil*, the chef's "transsubstantiations" are linked amusingly, without the slightest blasphemous intention, to the mystical transsubstantiation of the eucharist. In its hyperbolic evocations of the cook as a Vulcan in his forge, a sculptor, painter, potter, pianist, the novel raises Félicie's art to mock-heroic stature. In *A la recherche*, Françoise's genius, demonstrated especially in her boeuf en daube created in honor of M. de Norpois, is hymned with a restraint that lends greater authority to her creations' claim to the status of minor masterpieces. This claim receives a final and totally serious confirmation at the end of *Le Temps retrouvé*, where her boeuf à la mode is included in the famous series of analogies which recapitulates the creative filiation between the hero's book to come and its modest precursors.

These analogies may at first glance appear extravagant if one considers the minimal or at least utterly fragile form of a composition like Françoise's, which is doomed to obliteration by the first guest who serves himself. Yet their inclusion among the authentic pre-texts of the book to come is warranted by their substance and force, if not by their fragile form. An undue preoccupation with *A la recherche*'s own powerful formal unity may prevent the reader from noticing how consistently the hero, in assessing a composition's "truth," focuses his attention not on its formal finish, but on its power of transitivity whereby it brings to light new resources, new life-giving harmonies and makes them accessible to others. The perfect antithesis of Françoise's formally precarious but original and satisfying creations which grow directly out of the conjunction of her talents and the gifts of the seasons, is the salon which Mme Verdurin is laboring feverishly to distill to an ultimate exclusiveness. Odette envies her art, "those arts to which the Mistress attached such paramount importance, although they did no more than discriminate between shades of the non-existent, sculpture the void, and were, strictly speaking, the Arts of Nonentity: to wit those, in the lady of a house, of knowing how to bring people together, how to 'group,' to draw out, to 'keep in the background,' to act as a 'connecting link' " (1:647; 1:601).

Between the two extremes of an empty, intransitive form devoid of life, and creations like Françoise's that are rich in substance but of such immediate transitivity that they are reabsorbed by life almost at the moment of their completion, *A la recherche* inscribes in its hero's inner book sketches from the arts of life that achieve to an at least minimal degree that fusion of substance and form, intimacy and distance, that marks the compositions of the masters. The most resplendent of these are the creations of Odette. Banal, ignorant and superstitious in her beliefs, ideas and social ambitions, untruthful and unfaithful in her relationships with men, mediocre in almost every way, Odette reveals herself to be an authentic artist and creator of happiness in at least one area of her life. In her threefold creation of a radiantly beautiful face out of a drawn and almost ugly one, the poetic setting of her salon with its "winter garden" and superb chrysanthemums and, above all, the unique elegance of her clothes that make her the queen of the springtime Bois de Boulogne, she proves herself to be the composer of works of beauty of at least seasonal duration. In a note written in 1915 in reply to a question about Odette's fortunes, Proust not only informed his correspondent that Odette had become more beautiful still (despite the fact that she was no longer young), but summarized the process whereby she had transformed her irregular, unreliable features—her sallow complexion and weary, drawn face that used so often to disappoint Swann—into a face of "eternal youthfulness."

That "eternally youthful" face, far from being a gift of nature, is a conscious creation which triumphs over the fluctuations of mood, energy and, above all, time, and "uncovers" an even, radiant and immutable face. Furthermore, with the fortune that her marriage to the rich Swann has placed at her disposal, Odette is able to extend the scope of her talents. Freed from the uncertainties of the courtesan's life and from the bad, pseudo-exotic taste of her apartment on the rue La Pérouse which still reflected the cocotte rather than the individual woman, encouraged also by Swann's artistic taste, she creates in their elegant salon an ambiance of voluptuousness, delicacy and mystery which not only bears a close affinity to certain aspects of Bergotte's novels, but which becomes for Bergotte himself a source of delight and inspiration. Odette may be stupidly mistaken in her claim that she is "guiding" Bergotte with her advice, but "[It] must be admitted that she did inspire him, though not in the way that she supposed. But when all is said there are, between what constituted the elegance of Mme Swann's drawing room and a whole aspect of Bergotte's work, connections such that either of them might serve, among elderly men today, as a commentary upon the other" (1:604; 1:561).

The poetic, dreamy salon which inspires not only Bergotte but also and above all the adolescent hero who feels transported by it even as he smarts from Gilberte's rejection, derives its charm from the artful correspondences which Odette has created between the furniture, from the Louis XV armchairs in pale pink silk to the copper red samovar, and the fragile chrysanthemums whose hues reflect the same palette. These correspondences so excite the hero's imagination that on its own it extends them by another octave as it were, to the delicate sunset in the November sky outside. The three registers repeating the same *motif*, the inanimate and closed world of period objects, the wholly evanescent vision of the sunset and, mediating between them, enlivening the former and domesticating the latter and giving it substance, the vibrant flowers, succeed the "octaves" of Saint-Hilaire and Giverny in a series of harmonic figures which the apprentice writer's sensibility registers as major metaphors of "translation."

Odette is far from being the only character in *A la recherche* whose creative talents are the "other" side of an ordinary and at least partly detestable self. Albertine is another, and so is the friend of Vinteuil's daughter, who may have hastened the father's death by the grief she caused him but who, a splendid musician herself and former pupil of his, has with supreme dedication and musicianly instinct transcribed the master's almost illegible manuscript of the septet and given it to the world. So are Morel the blackmailer, tramp and incomparable violinist; Rachel, cheap prostitute—the "Rachel quand du Seigneur" who drove Saint-Loup to thoughts of suicide—and successor of the great Berma; Octave the loafer, gambler, upstart golfer of Balbec, whose stage designs astound the hero years later by their originality. And closest of all to "pure nature," there are those untutored rhapsodists, the two sisters and "couriers" at the Grand Hôtel, Marie Gineste and Céleste Albaret—"Ah, sac à ficelles, ah! douceur, ah! perfidie! rusé entre les rusés, rosse des rosses! Ah! Molière!"—"who had learned absolutely nothing at school, and yet whose language was somehow so literary that, but for the almost wild naturalness of their tone, one would have thought their speech affected." His inner sketchbook preserves all of these, and many more, carefully. But to Odette's works the cycle accords a special place.

Alone in *A la recherche*, Odette is both creator and creation, a living paradigm of that imbrication of art and life which the hero's imagination keeps seeking out. In her fervently anticipated, always sudden and miraculous emergence on the Avenue du Bois on Sundays shortly after noon, in her gowns of delicate mauve and her smile, she is a being belonging to "another race," whose air of calm sovereignty, freedom and happiness marks an artist sure of her powers. The art which sets her gown with its accessories and parasol apart from those of all the other elegant women is "connected with the season and the hours by a bond both necessary and unique" and creates the illusion of a naturalness more natural than that of the real flowers of May. It is supremely attuned to the given—a period style, a season, the mood and temperature of the hour, yet at the same time unique in the choice and blending of its materials. And like the art of the masters it is wholly disinterested, applying its fine craftsmanship to the most minute and hidden details:

> ... I would discover in the blouse ... a thousand details of execution which had had every chance of remaining unobserved, like those parts of an orchestral score to which the composer has devoted infinite labour although they may never reach the ears of the public: or in the sleeves of the jacket that lay folded

across my arm I could see . . . some exquisite detail, a delicately tinted strap, a lining of mauve satinette which, ordinarily concealed from every eye, was yet as delicately fashioned as the outer parts, like those Gothic carvings on a cathedral, hidden on the inside of a balustrade eighty feet from the ground, as perfect as the bas-reliefs over the main porch . . . (1:686; 1:638).

None of the elements of Odette's art are lost on the hero. The "poetic sensation" engendered in him by her symphony in mauve of the noon hour in May, complementing her "Symphony in White" of Holy Week, transcends the hour and the season. They take their place in his sketchbook alongside Saint-Hilaire and alongside the many other fragile creations which point towards the book to come with the twofold power of artistic pre-texts and embodiments of moments of his past. That noon hour becomes one of the high moments on the metaphorical "sundial" into which *A la recherche* "translates" or, in truth, composes its hero's life: ". . . now that the sorrows that I once felt on Gilberte's account have long since faded and vanished, there has survived them the pleasure that I still derive—whenever I close my eyes and read, as it were upon the face of a sundial, the minutes that are recorded between a quarter past twelve and one o'clock in the month of May—from seeing myself once again strolling and talking thus with Mme Swann, beneath her parasol, as though in the coloured shade of a wistaria bower" (1:689-690; 1:641).

The movement of return of *A la recherche* to the pre-texts of the book to come is well designed, as George Stambolian has noted, "to call us back to life and to reveal in life the sources of art."[4] It is equally designed to uncover in art the source of new life and new works of art. The cycle's impact on its reader is remarkably like that of another of Proust's favorite painters, Chardin, on the writer himself. It does not undermine life, as Blanchot would have it who sees the text turning life's dense reality into the spectral irreality of its pages.[5] Rather, like Chardin's paintings it makes him return to life with an enhanced eagerness to "read" and redesign it:

The pleasure we get from his painting of a room in which someone is sewing, a pantry, a kitchen, a sideboard is, caught as it were in flight, detached from the moment, fathomed in depth, eternalized, the pleasure which he got out of a sideboard, a kitchen, a pantry, a room in which someone is sewing. They are so inseparable from one another that, if he was incapable of being satisfied with the first and wanted to give himself and others the second, you in turn will not be satisfied with the second and will return to the first. (*Essais et articles*, 373-374)

The passage's circular structure embodies perfectly this characteristically Proustian back and forth movement from text to living sketch or pre-text and back to and beyond the text. It is easy to see why a great Proust critic, Georges Poulet, first placed the stress on the retrospective movement of *A la recherche*,[6] to shift it in a later essay to the cycle's forward thrust.[7] The two are in fact wholly interrelated. An intimate link between the forward surge of anticipation and creative prescience and the backward-directed quest for beginnings marks both the hero's inner journey of consciousness and the unfolding of the text. As for the first, as Poulet has shown, no sooner are the hero's hopes of becoming a writer arrested by the disillusionments of adult life, than unexpected surges of the involuntary memory launch him on a new journey, now of retrospection, to recover the lost paradises of his childhood and youth. But no sooner launched, this journey, by leading him back into the heart of lost moments, revives his ardent anticipation of revelations to come that was those moments' hallmark, and propels him forward once again, now in determined pursuit of a vocation he long ago gave up as hopeless. The same basic back and forth rotation marks the text's own unfolding. What has been—the seemingly completed tale, and what is not yet—the book to come, are but dialectical moments in a narrative in which every return marks an advance towards an emerging yet ever elusive truth. In a way which ultimately transcends both past and future, the text revolves around a central, essential creative moment—always the same and each time different—in which a new way of seeing brings to light a new "translation" or new figure of truth.

3. "A Ray of Sunlight"

A la recherche is eloquent in persuading its reader that all human beings, real or fictional, carry within them an inner book as richly inscribed as its hero's. This may well be so. Other characters besides the hero love, hate, feel pangs of jealousy, enjoy Vermeer's paintings, Balzac's novels, Vinteuil's "white" sonata and "crimson" septet, and their favorite cities and landscapes. But if this means to suggest that they too could bring these impressions to light, "translate" them if only they were willing to make the effort, the reader cannot help but smile. One feels moved and bemused by the pedagogical strain in Proust's genius which led him, in a fictional sleight-of-hand, to evoke his hero's "reading" as a paradigm for any reader in pursuit of his own inner truth.

Things are not so simple, as the cycle makes abundantly clear. Not only may the most richly inscribed inner book remain buried in darkness if unprobed, its "negatives" left undeveloped as in Swann's life, but conversely, even the mind's most avid probings may fail to translate the inner book into the figures of a real one. Indeed a profound difference sets apart the Proustian metaphorical reading from a purely cognitive quest for truth. First and foremost, it is an act of creative passion. Passion alone, whether it is the passion for knowledge or its ostensible enemy and secret accomplice, desire,[1] is able to mobilize the mediating power without which no reading can turn life's opaque negatives into poetic truths. That mediator, the greatest, most magisterial power in Proust's tale of a book's genesis, both as a physical reality and as a metaphor, is the sun. The solar fire and light penetrate and dissolve all barriers, illuminate the innermost layers of the hidden, invisible script and activate its latent signs.

A great deal of stress has been placed on the Proustian image of the writer as recluse and on the prevalence in the cycle of enclosed, dark spaces—the shuttered room, the bed, the nest, Noah's Ark—which shelter the hero from the threats of the outside world as they heighten his power to draw the world into his own inner orbit.[2] Yet while withdrawal and silence did indeed mark the years of Proust's writing of *A la recherche*, and are beckoning to the hero at the end of the cycle so that he may begin to write *his* book, the book's genesis as it is evoked in *Contre Sainte-Beuve* and *A la recherche* is linked in the most intimate way to the stages of a natural harvest's underground seeding, budding and ripening in a sun which not merely nurtures, but which transforms even potentially destructive subterranean elements into creative forces expanding ever outward. In tracing the emergence of the hero's book back to its natural, non-literary pre-texts in life, the cycle presents the reader with a veritable "physiology of the book," in which the bond between life and the book, between natural sunlight and the metaphorical sunlight which "translates the world, " both inner and outer, is such that each depends on the other for sustenance and validation.

To begin as it were underground, the hero's inner book is the very antithesis of a Lockean *tabula rasa* which passively records and stores sensory impressions. It is volcanic in character and imparts its own latent violence of desire to every sign it registers.[3] Each of its multiple, seemingly petrified layers, which range from the fresh "negatives" of the present and immediate past to the deepest imprints of childhood, holds captive one of his innumerable successive selves. Yet, like volcanic strata, these layers are by no means as inert and separate as they appear. Repeatedly, in his life's privileged moments, they erupt with cataclysmic force and are transformed into a molten "lava." In a series of powerful organic metaphors which encompass geological cataclysms, sunlight and fire, electricity and sudden, explosive germinations, the texts evoke those moments of upheaval in which his whole being is galvanized out of the petrified state into which time has traduced it, and set free by "that enthusiasm, that mental renewal in which all partitions seem to tumble and no barrier, no rigidity remains in us, in which our whole substance seems a kind of lava ready to flow, to take whatever form we wish, and nothing in us remains as it was, to hold us back" (*Essais et articles*, 422).[4]

In those moments the self feels reprieved from its inarticulate existence whose variegated hours have merely displaced one another in its field of vision without any kind of meaningful interaction. In a flash, the self's somber vision of life or rather its inability to see anything in the press of the moment is transformed into a solar vision of limitless creative possibilities. As if by magic, it feels freed to seize itself in its totality, that is to say, to create itself anew by means of the concentrated power of the imagination— Baudelaire's "queen of the faculties"[5] which Proust, like his favorite poet, tends to equate with the power not of invention but of sensibility and memory.[6] And as the inner walls give way, the self feels reopened to the innumerable worlds of the non-self which have ceased to exist for it as time has amortized its curiosity and perceptions, and impelled to embrace them anew in an impulse that is reminiscent of Baudelaire's artistic—and divine—"prostitution." In their mediating power those annunciatory moments become paradigms for the sustained power of mediation vested in the book to come. Through it the dichotomy which rends apart the Proustian hero's self; namely, the split between what it perceives to be an enslaved and guilty self-in-the-world, and "another self," the only true one which, upon the death of the first, must translate life's aberrations into the truth of the book, is transcended.

Before going further, it may be important to try to understand what led Proust—and his hero—to maintain this dualist stance. Clearly the moralist strain in Proust was strong. Not only was it nurtured by a Catholic tradition which he had inherited from his father's side of the family (all of life in Combray gravitates around the church of Saint-Hilaire), and by a classical literary heritage which led him to discover early his deep affinities with the greatest Jansenist poet, Racine; but in a more immediate way, the emotional and sexual turmoil of his life which was threatening to undermine his creative will was bound to reinforce his somber view of human existence. The threat of damnation which hovers over the Cities of the Plain that increasingly dominate the Proustian landscape, bespeaks a moralist of Old Testament and Jansenist dimensions. But the immediate literary provocation for his insistence on the writer's divided self came from Sainte-Beuve and his positivist disciples. It is not difficult to see how offensive the misapplication of scientific determinism to literature must have been to a writer in whose texts the book is the supreme figure of human freedom. In *Contre Sainte-Beuve* Proust scores the fallaciousness of a biographical method which not merely confused the writer with the perishable, idiosyncratic, flawed man—Stendhal with Henri Beyle—, but accorded primacy to the latter since, instead of seeking the design of the writer's life in his texts, it sought to decipher the texts by means of every available scrap of information about his life.

Examples of the radical difference in quality between the artist's "other self" and his self-in-the-world abound in *A la recherche*. The adolescent hero is crushed when he finally encounters his idol Bergotte, "le doux chantre," in the form of a pretentious young man with a seashell nose, black goatee and an affected way of speaking who, furthermore, as he finds out a little later, is not above saying nasty things about his friends. In *A l'ombre des jeunes filles*, still not having learned the lesson that the artist's creative self is not the same as that of the man who is seen at parties, makes love, or ingratiates himself with those who can further his career, he is again bewildered to find out from Elstir that the vulgar, boisterous M. Biche whom Swann had to endure at the Verdurins' was the great painter himself as a young man. Swann in turn discards as laughable any suggestion that the composer of the divine sonata, whose identity he is trying to discover, might have been the prudish, timid piano teacher and disgraced father of Montjouvain whom he would greet with the special courtesy of condescension whenever he met him on the road. No wonder, Proust observes scathingly in *Contre Sainte-Beuve*, the critic was led to place Béranger above Baudelaire by asking such questions about his poet as: "What did he think of religion? How did the spectacle of nature affect him? How did he behave in regard to women? To money? Was he rich or poor? What was his daily diet? His routine? What was his vice or weakness?" "This method disregards what a deeper familiarity with our own self teaches us; namely, that a book is the product of another self than the one we display in our habits, in society, in our vices. That self, if we want to understand it, it is only in our innermost being and through the effort of recreating it in ourselves that we can hope to do so. Nothing can dispense us from this effort of our heart. This is a truth we have to create in its entirety." Even after Sainte-Beuve's life had become a life of steady, arduous writing, Proust goes on to say, he would "continue to fail to understand that unique world, closed, without communication with the outside, that is a poet's soul" (Pléiade ed., 221-225).

But, "without communication with the outside . . . .?" This is a perplexing claim by the composer of a text in which inside and outside, surfaces and depth, the noisy, busy self-in-the-world and the silent "other self" are engaged with one another to the point where the dividing line between them becomes ultimately as invisible as the line between land and sea in Elstir's "Port de Carquethuit." Throughout the hero's long journey of apprenticeship in which, as Charles Du Bos said of Baudelaire's, no in-between state seems possible between total misery and total happiness, the book to come can be seen opening up an inner distance in which the disparate elements of his experience assume beauty and meaning in the light of his deep self's power of reflection. However sharply the tale seeks to divide its hero's destiny temporally into a blindly lived existence and the hero-turned-narrator's retrospective illumination of that existence in a spectral afterlife, vision cannot be said to succeed blindness even in his own life, and even less so in the lives of the cycle's other, active composers. For already throughout its prolonged period of gestation, the book he carries within him draws forth the multiple moments of recognition in which an involuntary memory, a wholly anticipatory intimation or an intellectual perception grasps an analogy, or a poetic sensation apprehends behind an object the promise of "another" world or, more starkly, the unfathomable mystery of time's own creations. Long before it is to be written, its volume *is* that inner distance.[7]

Within it, both the worldly self and the "other" can be seen undergoing a significant change. What the book to come teaches the deep self is not to turn its back on the other to pursue an otherworldly truth of its own, but rather to seek to illuminate the shallow, disjointed surfaces of existence and give them depth through its reflective power. In *L'Etre et le néant*, Sartre illustrates the nature of this process on the cognitive level with the example of the crescent moon. Whereas the blind self sees only the crescent moon in its "thereness," the other perceives and reveals it in its incompleteness, thereby "realizing" its absent fullness. "What is released to intuition is an in-itself which by itself is neither complete nor incomplete but which simply is what it is, without relation with other beings. In order for this in-itself to be grasped as the crescent moon, it is necessary that a human reality surpass the given toward the project of the unrealized totality—here the disk of the full moon—and return toward the given to constitute it as the crescent moon; that is, in order to realize it into being in terms of the totality which becomes its foundation."[8] Its search, "down there, beyond its grasp, in the far reaches of possibility,"[9] takes the form in *A la recherche* of the deep self's rising to the challenge held out to it by the given. This, the hero learns in the course of his apprenticeship, is not a one-sided process. Just as vision opens up the opaque surfaces and sets them free to combine in new, mutually illuminating figures, so conversely the surfaces give solid anchor to a depth which would otherwise remain intangible and out of touch with existence. A wonderful example of this anchoring process can be found in the episode of his stay at Doncières in *Le côté de Guermantes*. Throughout his stay he is in a state of euphoria. The bracing sturdiness, bustle and camaraderie of military life in the barracks, some of which he is allowed to share with Saint-Loup and his friends, are captured in his metaphor of a deep-sea diver's lifeline to the surface: "Like a diver breathing through a pipe which rises above the surface of the water, I felt that I was in some sense linked to a healthy, open-air life through my connexion with those barracks, that towering observatory dominating a country-side furrowed with strips of green enamel, into whose various buildings I esteemed it a priceless privilege, which I hoped would last, to be free to go whenever I chose, always certain of a welcome" (2:94; 2:96).

Above all, the "other self" becomes able to recognize the inestimable contribution to its own quest by what it has tended to and continues to view as its most implacable enemy, belonging wholly to the self-in-the-world, namely, the body. It discovers the body's "other" side.[10] The same body which the hero perceives as the great seducer drawing him away from his vocation and which causes some of his deepest miseries, belongs also and in equal measure to the creative self. In its "other" role, it is the infallible, incorruptible, ever vigilant custodian of the inner book of his life, without which there could no more be a book than there could be a plant without a seed. ". . . this life of mine, the memories of its sadnesses and its joys, formed a reserve which fulfilled the same function as the albumen lodged in the germ cell of a plant, from which that cell starts to draw the nourishment which will transform it into a seed long before there is any outward sign that the embryo of a plant is developing, though already within the cell there are taking place chemical and respiratory changes, secret but extremely active. In the same way my life was linked to what eventually would bring about its maturation" (3:936; 3:899).

The hero's powerfully embodied self transcends from the cycle's very beginning any dichotomy between a self-in-the-world belonging wholly to desire, and "another," serving truth, since it alternately represents and acts on behalf of one *and* the other. On the one hand, he feels deeply threatened by his body. In the eccentricity of its desires, the aggressiveness of its claims which become more violent the more they are censured, it is a constant potential source of disaster, a tyrant enslaving the will, an obstacle in the self's quest for truth. It implicates the self in moral guilt; worse still, it blocks the inner visionary faculties which are struggling to come to the surface. But at the same time, this body— its senses, nerves, muscles, limbs—in registering all dimensions of his experience with infallible precision, is able to testify to the self's true condition, not only that of others, but his own, when all else— ideas, ambitions, desires, hopes, fears—lie to it and deceive it. As in the fictional lives created by another great seer of the flesh, Tolstoy, in which Natasha's wild shrieks during the hunt, Anna's lowered eyelids, or the groans of the dying Ivan Ilytch, reveal their untamed passion, self-deception or revolt, so in *A la recherche*, the decipherer learns to read the body's language, including his own, which signals with a power that strips bare the deepest levels of the unconscious, the truth about the self's freedom or enslavement. With a directness that instantaneously reveals the falsehood of the words proffered, Legrandin's transfixed glance and M. de Charlus' high-pitched voice give the lie to their vehement verbal assertions of freedom from the "sin without remission" of snobbishness or from effeminacy.

Especially, again in a manner reminiscent of Tolstoy, the future writer's body becomes a supreme awakener of consciousness through its seemingly unlimited capacity for suffering. Pain reveals to him spontaneously and with imperious power the gaping discrepancy between truth and illusion or, to underscore the link between them, the truth *about* illusion. Stunned by Françoise's announcement: "Mlle Albertine has left," he can only marvel at the power of the sharp pain which suddenly takes his breath away to dispel his illusion that he has grown tired of Albertine, and to "crystallize" the truth of his desperate attachment to the fugitive girl:

> Yes, a moment ago, before Françoise came into the room, I had believed that I no longer loved Albertine, I had believed that I was leaving nothing out of account, like a rigorous analyst; I had believed that I knew the state of my own heart. But our intelligence, however lucid, cannot perceive the elements that compose it and remain unsuspected so long as, from the volatile state in which they generally exist, a phenomenon capable of isolating them has not subjected them to the first stages of solidification. I had been mistaken in thinking that I could see clearly into my own heart. But this knowledge, which the shrewdest perceptions of the mind would not have given me, had now been brought to me, hard,

glittering, strange, like a crystallized salt, by the abrupt reaction of pain. (3:426; 3:420)

The body's role in the genesis of the book extends further yet. An abundance of metaphors depict it as a mediator in one of the most far-reaching and fruitful Proustian relationships of all, namely, that between the creative self and the natural world. To begin with, there is a ceaseless exchange of energy between the two.[11] How deeply the fecundity of the hero's imagination depends on this exchange can be seen in the *leitmotiv*, which runs through several of the texts, of the little mannikin in the optician's shop window. Sprung from his father's keen but, as befits his character, "scientific" interest in meteorology, the mannikin embodies the hero's own physiological responses, more powerful and abiding than any other, to the waxing and waning of light and the seasons. Totally antithetical in spirit to Baudelaire's celebration of the sun in "Paysage" or "Le Soleil"[12] with its Symbolist polarity of the inner "soleil de mon coeur," symbol of the poet's power and will to transfigure the world, and the outer world of nature (the stormy night which rages outside the poet's window), the little capucin is sustained by and fully in tune with all the shades and gradations of natural sunlight:

> ... knowing that he would make me happier than Albertine, I remained closeted with the little person inside me, the melodious hymner of the rising sun .... Of the different persons that compose our personality, it is not the most obvious that are the most essential. In myself, when ill health has succeeded in uprooting them one after another, there will still remain two or three endowed with a hardier constitution than the rest, notably a certain philosopher who is happy only when he has discovered between two works of art, between two sensations, a common element. But I have sometime wondered whether the last of all might not be this little mannikin, very similar to another whom the optician at Combray used to set up in his shop window to forecast the weather, and who, doffing his hood when the sun shone, would put it on again if it was going to rain.... I dare say that in my last agony, when all my other 'selves' are dead, if a ray of sunshine steals into the room while I am drawing my last breath, the little barometric mannikin will feel a great relief, and will throw back his hood to sing: " Ah! Fine weather at last!" (3:4; 3:12)

This intense interaction between sunlight and the writer's self no matter how ailing, is more than an influx of vital emergy from one into the other. Long before the hero's mind will discern his vocation with any clarity (he still thinks that literature is *mimesis*, based on observation or, alternately, that it is composed with clever ideas), a ray of sunlight presents him with an "artistic composition" which his senses have no trouble whatever registering as a natural paradigm of his book to come. The episode (an earlier and weaker version of which is "Le rayon de soleil sur le balcon" in *Contre Sainte-Beuve*) occurs in *Du côté de chez Swann* and is but one of countless deceptively realistic Proustian episodes which conceal their metaphorical design. What it evokes is not just the sunlight's psychological effect, its power to revive the adolescent's disconsolate spirits, but its "artistic" power to recompose an unsatisfactory external reality of purely contiguous, unrelated surfaces, and give it coherence and meaning. A gloomy, heavily overcast morning which has been threatening to keep the hero from finding Gilberte on the Champs-Elysées, is suddenly transformed into a blissful morning of hope by a shaft of sunlight which has alighted on the balcony wall. In the metamorphosis produced by the light, the balcony's dull surfaces of stone and iron railing become translucent and compose themselves into a deep, velvety volume in which their distinctive contours, far from being effaced, are brought out in sharp relief. In the sunlight's action, from its first hesitant stirring and vacillations, to its increasingly powerful pulsations and final "artistic" triumph, the young hero reads so precise a metaphorical prefiguration of the art of "translation," that despite its length the passage warrants quoting in its entirety:

> ... if it rained, what was the use of going to the Champs-Elysées? And so, from lunch-time onwards, my anxious eyes never left the unsettled, clouded sky. It remained dark. the balcony in front of the window was grey. Suddenly, on its sullen stone, I would not exactly see a less leaden colour, but I would feel as it were striving towards a less leaden colour, the pulsation of a hesitant ray that struggled to discharge its light. A moment later, the balcony was as pale and luminous as a pool at dawn, and a thousand shadows from the iron-work of its balustrade had alighted on it. A breath of wind would disperse them, the stone darkened again, but, as though they had been tamed, they would return; imperceptibly, the stone whitened once more, and as in one of those uninterrupted crescendos, which in music, at the end of an overture, carry a single note to the supreme fortissimo by making it pass rapidly through all the intermediate stages, I would see it

reach that fixed, unalterable gold of fine days, on which the clear-cut shadow of the wrought iron of the balustrade was outlined in black like some capricious vegetation, with a delicacy in the delineation of its smallest details that seemed to indicate a deliberate application, an artist's satisfaction, and with so much relief, so velvety a bloom in the restfulness of its dark, felicitous masses that in truth those broad and leafy reflections on that lake of sunshine seemed aware that they were pledges of tranquillity and happiness. (1:429-430; 1:396)

The sunlight's composition explains nothing and it has nothing to do with the retrospective illuminations of memory. Rather, it weaves a new constellation of harmony that is all its own. But that makes its lesson in composition all the clearer. What it illuminates for the budding writer is the fundamental law of Proustian composition, regardless of whether it is a "reading" or deciphering of truth or a wholly prospective creation: nothing about this world, not the slightest detail is changed by it; yet everything is changed. All the surface realities are there, familiar, seemingly untouched; but now their natural appearance is marked by an indefinable yet unmistakable difference. Their naturalness, a quality so admired by the hero's grandmother as a mark of the highest truth both in life and in art, is no longer given but created. This higher naturalness both conceals and reveals a new, "other" dimension which sets apart the recomposed things from the purely natural ones, as the church of Saint-Hilaire, for all its unassuming simplicity, is felt by everyone in Combray to belong to a different world than Mme. Loiseau's house which adjoins it, no matter how unabashedly her fuchsias climb over and onto the church's venerable walls. What the hero's sensibility registers in the composition he has before his eyes is its complete freedom from arbitrariness. Nothing is fabricated. The sunlight's "artistic conscientiousness and application" works on what is given—the physical elements of the balcony and the adolescent's emotions—without suppressing any of their individual attributes. It renders translucent and draws together the disparate elements that fall within its orbit and transfigures them as it were from within through its own reflecting power. The happiness the ray of sunlight creates here can be seen emanating from all compositions in *A la recherche*, humble or great, and is felt by all of the cycle's composers, no matter how arduous their labors.[13]

Finally, the sunlight inscribes in the hero's inner book a last crucial lesson in artistic integrity. Subject like all participants in the natural cycle of life, death and rebirth to the principle of intermittency, the sunlight can compose a balcony or a seascape at Balbec only during certain hours. In between these, its power must yield to the darkness of night as well as to clouds and rain. And when its power to illuminate and compose things is thus held in abeyance, when it cannot see anything, metaphorically speaking, its truth becomes just that inability to see. The hero's creative self, rooted as it is in its physical responses to the world, is subject to the same intermittency. Until such a time, which lies well beyond the end of the cycle's last chapter, when the "magnetizing" power of his pen may become able to translate this very intermittency into one of the book's major truths, he too must accept his moments of blindness and resist the temptation, when he cannot see, to fabricate a false completeness. Jean Santeuil learned this lesson from the Monets, in which the limited range of light and the presence of a fog which the sun is unable to dispel become metaphors of life's instability, the precariousness of forms and the limits of vision, and hence, new painterly truths of the highest order. Unlike Monet and the mature writer of *A la recherche*, the young Marcel Proust had not yet mastered the art of composing a unified fictional volume out of his discontinuous moments of vision, but he proved his artistic integrity by not concealing the blanks and discrepancies between them. All of Jean's superabundant moments of insight—whether of introspection, reflections about the writer's vocation, sensory epiphanies, perception of other characters or of the subtle gradations of falsehood in the social sphere—remain unconnected. As Maurice Blanchot has said of *Jean Santeuil*, its empty spaces simply remain empty; they do not function.[14] The work is a series of unrelated tableaux and privileged moments. It is not yet a book in the full Proustian sense.

Several years later, *Contre Sainte-Beuve* evokes directly that discouraging alternation in the narrator's self between vision and blindness, which for him mean life and death, which leads him to compare himself to a seed which alternately thrives and withers. A glimpse of an analogy between two things brings him to life, only to leave him to die again in those moments of blindness when reality falls apart once more into unrelated particulars. Soon, he tells himself, it will be too late; his "other self," weakened by the drought of his life, will be silenced forever. And yet,

... an idea resurrects it, like those seeds which stop sprouting when the air is too dry, but which a little humidity and warmth is sufficient to restore to life. And I think that the fellow inside me who spends his time this way must be the same one who also has a sharp, finely attuned ear which can perceive between two impressions, two ideas a very subtle harmony that others do not perceive. I have no idea who this creature may be. But if in a sense he creates those harmonies, they in turn bring him to life; right away he rises up, buds, grows with the life they give him, and then dies, being able to live only through them.... But the time he lives, his life is nothing but ecstasy and happiness. He alone should be writing my books.
(Fallois ed., 359-360)

But of course he alone cannot. The book as "sundial" or revelation of hidden correspondences must inscribe within itself its own limit and contradiction. The other side of the "sundial" truth of *A la recherche* is that of a kaleidoscopic whirl of errant constellations resisting all deciphering. It demands another, wholly immanent kind of composing which, akin to nature's ray of sunlight, fashions unity out of strictly heterogeneous elements.

II.

The Text: Two-in-One

In a unique way, *A la recherche* presents itself to the reader as two texts in one, not consecutive like Vinteuil's sonata and septet, but unfolding simultaneously one within the other. The first, deeply rooted in an orphic tradition and structured by repetition, is a luminous book of hours. In the course of the cycle's slow gyrations, each essential hour or season of the hero's destiny which has first surged up with startling fortuitousness becomes familiar as it recurs in an ever extending chain of variations, and is ultimately captured in an allegorical figure that is as immutable as Giotto's Vices and Virtues in the Arena Chapel. In this book of hours, a realistic tale full of huge temporal gaps is transformed into a closed, unified metaphorical system of infinite reflectiveness and, at the furthest height of sublimation and abstraction, into the modern counterpart of an allegorical vision. However, even though ostensibly born of the same faith which illuminated the orphic seekers of the Platonic-Plotinian tradition, the Proustian book of hours presents itself as a precarious creation. Woven together by a supreme artistic effort, it is fated to show the ultimate truth of life eluding it as surely as Albertine breaks out of the prison in which an anxious lover has kept her and himself in bondage, and to make way for a new and different design. Through a continuous subversion of its "timeless" vision, it brings to the fore another which, like a plane redescending to earth, steers the reader back into time and the anguish of unanswered questions.

A la recherche might well be named "The Life, Death and Rebirth of Forms." It is all at once a celebration of the book's power to illuminate life and, in keeping with its own truth that "all is double" in life as in art, an unmasking of that power's potential transgression against life, which may lead not to the illumination but to the imprisonment of living forms. In the light of the gap kept open in the cycle between a finished tale and a still unwritten book, and of the signal role it assigns to the reader, first in the person of the hero who must decipher existence, then of the reader who must decipher the text, the allegorical vision which *A la recherche* ascends to can be no more than a privileged moment in the reader's journey. It is a "star" which enraptures him and guides him, but which cannot be the journey's end. For no sooner has a figure in the text captured the essence of a thing, than the latter breaks out of that figure's prison in search of a new and truer embodiment. Not only must Albertine, having emerged out of the nebulous cluster of the little band in *A l'ombre des jeunes filles* to become goddess and allegory in *La Prisonnière*, dissolve back into an intangible blur in *La Fugitive*, thus spurring the hero on in his pursuit of his elusive destination, but analogously, albeit on a different level since its identity is not obliterated, Vinteuil's white sonata too must yield, both in the composer's evolution and in the hearer's experience, to the somberer, more mysterious septet and its dissonances.

The hermetic book of revelation and the open book of questions that challenge each other in *A la recherche* are as inseparable as Vinteuil's sonata and septet or *La Prisonnière* and *La Fugitive*, the two volumes which may go further toward letting the reader in on the secret workings of the Proustian text than the explicit, almost didactic final meditations in *Le Temps retrouvé*. Like Vinteuil's two compositions, so the two volumes evoke the two sides, all at once contradictory and complementary, of the Proustian vision of the book:

> ... those two very dissimilar questions that governed the very different movements of the sonata and the septet, the former interrupting a continuous pure line, the latter welding together into an indivisible structure a medley of scattered fragments— one so calm and shy, almost detached and somewhat philosophical, the other so restless, urging, imploring—were nevertheless the same prayer, bursting forth like different inner sunrises and merely refracted through the different mediums of other thoughts, of artistic researches carried on through the years in which he had sought to create something new. (3:257; 3:255)

The two sides are again placed *en abyme* in *La Prisonnière*, the volume which constitutes by itself a cycle within the cycle. Opening on a radiant sunlit morning which allows the hero's imagination to take flight, and closing on an ominous moonlit morning that spells death, it describes perfectly both the promise and the failure of the lover's and would-be writer's quest to bring his Eurydice to light. It is a quest that leads first through metaphor, linked to the life-giving realm of the sun; then, in his despair over metaphor's powerlessness to redeem her, to the stillness of allegory, belonging to the cold star of night. In *La Prisonnière* a hidden link becomes visible between the lover's consuming passion to know and to possess the beloved, which turns life into "ashes," and the sublimated passion of the cycle's artists, the budding writer among them, whom the solar fire serves both as light in their quest for truth and as fire in their forge, but which may in its own turn threaten to destroy what it seeks to redeem.

Thus the figure of Albertine is far more than simply the antithesis of the hero's book to come. Underneath the very real opposition between the lover's destructive quest and the poet's self- and world-redeeming one, the text uncovers striking intertwinings. Already the hero's pursuit of Albertine has, for all its erotic frenzy, the hallmarks of a literary quest. Not only does the text accentuate the profusion of artistic analogies, metaphors and allegorical figures it elicits from him, as well as allusions to and *pastiches* of *Phèdre* and *Esther*, echoes of Baudelaire's "Invitation au voyage"—"ma soeur, mon enfant"—and reenactments of *Arabian Nights* conjurings, characters and settings; but, above all, it evokes the myth of Orpheus, casting Albertine in the role of not merely the beloved who causes her lover's despair, but of the poet's muse and his elusive creation. This fearsome love story may be a cautionary tale which bears not only on the dangers of love, but also on the dangers inherent in the decipherings of the book to come. If it depicts the lover's deadly venture to capture and possess the longed-for, elusive and unknowable Albertine as redeemable only by the book to come, it suggests, conversely, that the truth-quester's decipherings retain something of the powerlessness, even deadliness, of the lover's. At moments it seems as if one can virtually be read for the other, as when, through the whirling profusion of metaphors through which the hero has sought to capture the secret of Albertine's life, he flings her into the lofty sphere of pure allegory which threatens to immobilize her and causes her to flee for her life.[1] The abstract vision in azure and gold which he has superimposed on her proves indeed to be deadly: "I kissed her then a second time, pressing to my heart the shimmering golden azure of the Grand Canal and the mating birds, symbols of death and resurrection. But for the second time, instead of returning my kiss, she withdrew with the sort of instinctive and baleful obstinacy of animals that feel the hand of death" (3:406; 3:399).

His quest to wrest Albertine out of the shadows of real life is sharply arrested; its vertical movement turns into a descent back to level ground and pure metonymy. This reversal is signaled by a poignant metaphorical scene: the joyful crow of the cock has yielded to the melancholy cooing of the pigeons, as profoundly and mysteriously linked in its "lateral plaint" to the former's heaven-bound call as the septet's adagio to the allegro of its introduction and finale: "Likewise, this melancholy refrain performed by the pigeons was a sort of cockcrow in the minor key, which did not soar up into the sky, did not rise vertically, but, regular as the braying of a donkey, enveloped in sweetness, went from one pigeon to another along a single horizontal line, and never raised itself, never changed its lateral plaint into that joyous appeal which had been utered so often in the allegro of its introduction and finale . . . . I knew that I then uttered the word 'death,' as though Albertine were about to die" (3:408; 3:400-401).

Each time it approaches that limit where the book of revelation threatens to become a transgression against life and hence a falsehood, *A la recherche* converts itself with unsurpassed probity into a book of questions.

4. A Book of Hours

Two metaphors by means of which the cycle evokes the budding writer's premonitory joy of vanquishing time, namely his "reading" on the inner "sundial" of memory the magical minutes between a quarter past twelve and one o'clock in the month of May, embodied in the vision of Mme Swann emerging under her parasol on the Avenue du Bois, provide a key to the reader's own paradoxical delight in reading the entire *A la recherche*, surely one of literature's most relentless "comedies" since Dante's great poem and Balzac's *Comédie humaine*. They also help him to understand why his delight is so much more sustained than the hero's. For the latter, still deeply caught up in the currents of his constantly shifting feelings and desires, feels joy only in those intermittent moments in which either a "poetic sensation" or an epiphany of the involuntary memory triumphs over anguish by transporting him into "pure time." The reader's delight, on the other hand, is complete. What he is reading is not just a luminous hour here or season there that has surged up out of life's darkness and flux. He is reading a fictional cycle which, having fastened its thread in the daily recurring, dreaded evening hour in which the child is sent upstairs to bed or, as it seems to him, into the tomb, gradually weaves its way around all the crucial hours and seasons of his life and, in the course of its revolutions, transforms itself into an allegorical book of hours, in which "the whole world is merely a vast sun-dial, a single sunlit segment of which enables us to tell what time it is . . ." (3:638; 3:623). On this sundial not only the springtime and summer seasons, embodied in Combray and Balbec, are transfused with light, but even the infernal hours of desire and its delusions, which prevail almost unchallenged from *Du côté de Guermantes* to the final part of *Le Temps retrouvé*, are bathed in the refracted light of an ever-present even when invisible sun, which reveals their "lies and errors" as an essential truth of human nature.

This orphic sundial is clearly both vision and artifice. It embodies a profound vision of human existence by an artist who in his book turned "towards Apollo the sun god, that is to say, towards the work of creation in the light."[1] It is also the artful *Arabian Nights* face of *A la recherche*. Like Scheherazade who saved her life by the thread of her tales, so Proust wove out of a mere handful of his hero's death-bound hours an all-redeeming, golden cycle of eternal recurrence in which "everything must return in time, as it is written beneath the vaults of Saint Mark's, and proclaimed, as they drink from the urns of marble and jasper of the Byzantine capitals, by the birds which symbolize at once death and resurrection" (3:375-376; 3:368). The birds of Saint Mark become the emblem of the cycle's great law of recurrence: each crucial hour of the hero's life dies, only to be reborn in ever more decipherable guises, until at last, transcending its successive incarnations, it becomes a quintessential figure in the sundial's round.

The law of repetition is revealed by *A la recherche* to be the law of life. Simultaneously, in a text which consistently seeks to share with its reader the secret of its own workings, it reveals itself as the highest law of artistic creation.

"Life is a repetition and this is the beauty of life," Kierkegaard wrote in *The Repetition*, and added, "The love of repetition is the only happy love."[2] The "sundial" face of Proust's novel echoes this love. A modern counterpart of the traditional mystical path to illumination which conquers time and death, the Proustian repetition marks the stages of a spiritual apprenticeship which, however deeply rooted it may be in neurotic compulsion,[3] transcends compulsion to become a privileged means of vision. Repetition alone allows each moment of experience to be all at once integrated into the totality of the writer's unique, personal world and translated into a universal and universally recognizable figure.

The book of hours' intricate design appears to reflect so completely life's own truth that its effect is one of an enchanting naturalness. And that design—a round of figures of heaven, hell, purgatory and limbo, revolving on a sundial of blissful mornings, desolate evenings, the empty hours of worldly distraction and the "timeless" hours of memory and poetic sensations—is linked by the text to the truth-reflecting inner sphere of its hero's consciousness. In the latter's fiery mirror, life, transformed into a *cosa mentale*, becomes a dance in which the same figures keep recurring and intertwining. Childhood prescience seeds the ground for the aging man's reminiscence, the first working forwards, the second backwards, both divining the essential message of moments that are slated to return again and again.[4] By the same law which empowered Marcel Proust in an act of artistic prescience to conceive the beginning and the end of his cycle simultaneously, his young hero's prescience registers his great-aunt's cruelty in tempting the grandfather to drink the forbidden brandy as a prophetic scene, the first in a chain of moments of cruelty, his own and that of others, that will be as long as life itself. Throughout the cycle, it is prescience, so the tale persuades us, which leads him with infallible precision to the right spot at the right moment—at the risk of revealing that the all too human side of this *voyant* is a *voyeur*—to witness a truth-revealing recurrence. Thus the profanation scene of Montjouvain will be illuminated for him retrospectively by the scene of the baron de Charlus' first encounter with and wooing of Jupien in the courtyard of the Guermantes and, at last, by its grimmest double, the flagellation scene in Jupien's Temple de l'Impudeur in the blacked-out Paris of World War I. But not only does he discover in recurrence the essential identity of clearly similar hours. In the textual mirror's "magical simultaneities,"[5] life's seeming opposites as well, such as profanation and veneration, derangement and genius, the blind hours of erotic passion and the luminous hours of contemplation in turn intersect and cast light on each other, for "the coupling of contrary elements is the law of life, the principle of fertilization" (3:103; 3:108). This interplay of opposites may be a cause of anguish to the lover, but to the seeker of knowledge it is bliss. Each hour becomes an "annunciation" of an unchanging truth. Ultimately, each becomes as interchangeable with its precursors and successors as the countless scullery maids that have gone into the immutable figure of "Giotto's Charity" in Françoise's kitchen: "The kitchen-maid was an abstract personality, a permanent institution to which an invariable set of functions assured a sort of fixity and continuity and identity throughout the succession of transitory human shapes in which it was embodied; for we never had the same girl two years running" (1:86; 1:80).

This is the beauty of life, the book of hours tells the reader, that all is recurrence, essential oneness, that differences are but a transitory illusion. No sooner has the hero's grandmother died, than grief over her death begins to strip away from her daughter all that was merely her own, to bring to the fore so complete an identity between the two women that they merge in his mother into a single figure. The joyous morning hour which finds him in bed in the opening pages of *La Prisonnière*, sure of his captive and hence free to "read" in the "gospel of the day" that hour's unvarying message, confirms the blissful discovery of identity which endows each hour lived in time with an eternal presence:

> ... If I had not gone out with Albertine on her long expedition, my mind would stray all the further afield, and, because I had refused to savour with my senses this particular morning, I enjoyed in imagination all the similar mornings, past or possible, or more precisely a certain type of morning of which all those of the same kind were but the intermittent apparition which I had at once recognized; for the sharp wind blew the book open of its own accord at the right page, and I found before me, already marked, so that I might follow it from my bed, the Gospel for the day. This ideal morning filled my mind full of a permanent reality, identical with all similar mornings, and infected me with a joyousness which my physical debility did not diminish . . . ." (3:18; 3:26)

But it is in the sublime identity, even "monotony" of a great artist's creations that the truth and beauty of repetition are revealed to him in its fullness, both in its fusing of like and like and in its linking of opposites. First, as he hears one phrase, then another of the earlier sonata reappearing in the septet, each time in a new guise, he recognizes in the recurring phrases the "fairies, dryads and divinities" of Vinteuil's universe: ". . . again and again one phrase or another from the sonata recurred, but altered each time, its rhythm and harmony different, the same and yet something else, as things recur in life . . ." (3:261; 3:259). In turn, each recurring phrase calls forth others that sharply contrast with it; some joyous, some mysterious, others painfully strident, "which became in their turn seductive and persuasive as soon as they were tamed, and took their places in the round, the divine round that yet remained invisible to the bulk of the audience . . ." (3:261; 3:260).

The attractiveness and persuasiveness of each phrase of the septet, as of each hour and season of *A la recherche*, no matter how distressing its character at first and perceived in isolation, hinges on its recurrence and participation in the "divine round." Each time it recurs, its essential message becomes more transparent. At the same time, as it revolves with and around the other figures, a process of reciprocal modulation takes place in which, typically, the darkness of the nadir hour of profanation at Montjouvain is attenuated by the radiance of the zenith hour of the septet's first performance, made possible by Mlle Vinteuil's friend's transcription of the now dead composer's notebooks, or the hero's own profanation of his mother redeemed by his forthcoming "maternal" labors and sacrifices.[6]

The glory of the Proustian sundial, of which the divine round of the septet is a key metaphor, lies precisely in that movement of recurrence and in the metaphorical richness it produces. Like Vinteuil's phrases, its timeless hours retain enough of the individuality of their time-bound models to be filled to the brim with life. At the same time, the metaphorical modulations which each figure in the round undergoes opens up a process of reversibility: heaven, purgatory and hell are no longer the fixed, transcendent spheres of medieval theology, but the interacting, "interpolated" seasons of the pilgrim's life on earth, each of which can be redeemed by another in the flash of an illumination.

However, even as it weaves its round, the book of hours shows its reader the tenuousness of its glory and forces him to recognize the limit of its "eternalizing" power beyond which, as a modern text, it cannot go. As the cycle moves through the seer's own season in hell in *La Prisonnière*, in which life, embodied now in its totality in the figure of Albertine, presents itself to his blinded eyes as pure flux and inconstancy, its gyrations become frenzied to the point where it is thrust out of the vibrant solar sphere of metaphor which lies half-way between life's disorder and the disembodied unity of abstraction, into the moon-lit sphere of allegory. Many hundreds of pages earlier, the adolescent hero had a premonition of this danger. Looking out over the sea from Mme de Villeparisis's carriage which had stopped on a hill top, in *A l'ombre des jeunes filles*, he observed the "freezing" effect of a perspective that had grown too distant: ". . . I was no longer near enough to the sea, which seemed to me not alive but congealed; I no longer felt any power beneath its colours, spread like those of a picture between the leaves, through which it appeared as insubstantial as the sky and only of an intenser blue" (1:761; 1:708).

The allegorical thrust which makes of *A la recherche* a modern "Pilgrim's Progress"[7] is seen to culminate in a frozen emblematic figure in which the particular, unique reality of the original model or succession of models has been obliterated. In vain the quester and lover, drawn like Phèdre into a labyrinth, seeks to extricate both himself and the elusive beloved from it by endowing her, the labyrinth's shadowy center, with the depth and radiance of a "fixed star." When metaphors have proved unequal to the task of coordinating her disparate faces, and he is at last able to master the pulsations of anguish which produced their proliferation, he resorts to so detached a vision of love's sorrows and vanity that the figure it brings forth is as lifeless as the sea seen from the hill top. As he reflects in *La Fugitive* on the now distant season of his love for Albertine, no poetic sensation or involuntary memory, the text's two principal occasions for exuberant figurations, but a lofty intellectual vision which has won out over pain, extracts from that season an immutable, abstract emblem of "fixed gold and indestructible azure":

> ... much later, when I went back gradually, in reverse order, over the times through which I had passed before I had come to love Albertine so much, when my healed heart could detach itself from Albertine dead, then I was able to recall at length without suffering that day on which Albertine had gone shopping with Françoise instead of remaining at the Trocadéro; I recalled it with pleasure as belonging to an emotional season which I had not known until then; I recalled it at last exactly, no longer injecting it with suffering, but rather, on the contrary, as we recall certain days in summer which we found too hot while they lasted, and from which only after they have passed do we extract their unalloyed essence of pure gold and indestructible azure. (3:496; 3:486-487)

Like the hum of the engine that made possible a plane's ascent into the sky which he and Albertine had watched, spellbound, one day near La Raspelière, the almost neuralgic, pounding repetition of "Albertine... Albertine... Albertine... me rappeler... me rappelai... me rappelai... ce jour... ce jour... certains jours... sans souffrance... sans souffrance... souffrance... " may produce the detachment necessary to extract her "unalloyed essence," but the latter deprives her of life.

Nowhere in *A la recherche* is the link between desperation and abstraction more clearly visible, the roaring of the text's own engine as it rises above metaphor into the distilled realm of allegory more audible.[8] For in the lover's and putative writer's own season in hell in which "reading" is impossible, all of life becomes subsumed in the hollow, fleeting, colorful, unfathomable and deceitful phantom named Albertine. The young girl with the black polo cap, laughing eyes and rosy cheeks who first appeared to emerge out of the sea in the "nebula" of the little band in *A l'ombre des jeunes filles*, and was next seen wildly dashing off on her bicycle in all directions at once, a bird, a gull, a "luminous comet," and, in rare moments of repose, a harmonious Greek statue, becomes in *La Prisonnière*, as her mystery deepens in direct proportion to the hero's obsession with her, the embodiment of life's multiplicity and flux which resists all containment and can be subdued only by force.

> ... even allowing for her lies, it was incredible how spasmodic her life was, how fugitive her strongest desires.... And this instability of her feelings with regard to people, things, occupations, arts, places, was in fact so universal that, if she did love money, which I do not believe, she cannot have loved it for longer than anything else. When she said: Ah! If I had three hundred thousand francs a year! Or even if she expressed a nefarious but very short-lived thought, she could not have held on to it any longer than to the idea of going to Les Rochers, of which she had seen an engraving in my grandmother's edition of Mme de Sévigné, of meeting an old friend from the golf course, of going up in an aeroplane, of going to spend Christmas with her aunt, or of taking up painting again. (3:415-416; 3:408)

In their kaleidoscopic shifts, the metaphors and analogies designed to capture her tend on the contrary to cancel each other out to the point where neither the hero nor the reader is able to see her at all, even physically. For, "as soon as we have a desire to know, as the jealous man has, then it becomes a dizzy kaleidoscope in which we can no longer distinguish anything" (3:529; 3:519). In the frenzied process whereby they seek in vain to bestow form on her chameleon-like nature, she is made to traverse, like a comet, all of nature's spheres, all of the moral seasons and, finally, the supreme realm of artistic creation.

First, they link her to the unfathomable, unconscious realm of nature in the boundlessness of her amoral, purely instinctual appetites and movements. A creature of the sea the blue of which is reflected in her eyes, she is metamorphosed through a chain of similes and metaphors into a mysterious bird, a cruel gull in flight, a songbird whistling:

> For melancholy
> Is but folly,
> And he who heeds it is a fool. (3:3; 3:11)

a beautiful rose; in her sleep, into "a climbing plant, a convulvulus which continues to thrust out its tendrils whatever support you give it" (3:109; 3:113); finally, in her fateful imprisonment, into a domesticated animal in the form of a plump cat.

In the sphere of human passions, she becomes not only the supreme love object of his life, reducing her predecessors, Gilberte and Mme de Guermantes, and all other elusive objects of erotic passion in the cycle to mere "sketches" for her, but through her hinted at, but never fully proved association with Mlle Vinteuil and the actress Léa, she becomes the cycle's most shadowy and alluring androgyne and figure of Vice. This figure in turn is linked to a more worldly one which, in its pallor and black, evokes the image of the young Odette of the Paris demi-monde: "When Albertine came back to my room, she was wearing a black satin dress which had the effect of making her seem paler, of turning her into the pallid, intense Parisian woman, etiolated by lack of fresh air, by the atmosphere of crowds and perhaps by the practice of vice, whose eyes seemed the more uneasy because they were not brightened by any colour in her cheeks" (3:97; 3:102).[9]

Yet again, vice is only one of her many faces. She becomes the "fixed star" around which revolve all of the hero's moral seasons: a figure of paradise in the innocence of her sleep and her gay awakenings, in her gentle, sisterly attentiveness and, above all, through the "viaticum" of her good-night kiss which, in the "identical nature of the consolation" it bestows on him links her with the cycle's greatest figure of virtue, the hero's mother. She is a figure of purgatory in his tormented afternoon hours of uncertainty about her doings and true feelings, of limbo in the heavy dullness of her presence; of hell in the desolation before dawn and his near-certainty of her lies and lesbian betrayals.

Through an ever-expanding, seemingly uncontrollable chain of metaphorical, thematic, phonetic links, her image expands to the point where it encompasses every place, every moment, every sphere of his life, and in its ubiquitousness becomes as unfathomable as life itself. In the cycle's geography of time, it reaches from Balbec to Paris and Combray, from Nice to Touraine and, through the Fortuny gowns he has ordered for her, to the fabled Venice of oriental splendor which she has visited years before him and to which the need to guard her in captivity keeps him from journeying. She is linked to Bergotte and Gilberte by a syllable in her name; again to the latter in the thematic chains of love and androgyny; to Mlle Vinteuil in the spheres of lesbianism and music; she completes the chain of figures of elegance and sophistication which has led from Odette to the duchesse de Guermantes; she is the last link in a chain of deceitful mistresses. Finally and most importantly, her figure is linked to that of Elstir through the sea, her personal friendship with the painter and the great Venetian designer whom Elstir has discovered and whose clothes she wears; and, through the sonata and septet, to Vinteuil. Such is the hero's obsession to arrest her inconstancy and reduce her "otherness," that he attaches her systematically to the pursuit of his vocation. She displays a talent for painting; a "Saint Cecilia" at the piano, she becomes his muse by playing Vinteuil's music for him and inciting him to decipher the secrets of unfamiliar pieces; she becomes his "sister" and disciple in her literary talents—her stupendous rhapsody on ices is a strategically placed, wonderfully self-mocking parody of Proustian metaphor at its most extravagant. At last, having elicited from him crucial insights into the incomplete character of several modern masterpieces of literature and music, she becomes a prefiguration of his true Eurydice, his elusive book to come.

But his efforts to tie the numberless and conflicting threads converging in the "real" Albertine together into a unified creation prove futile. She is no longer a woman, but a being "scattered in space and time, . . . a series of events on which we can throw no light, a series of insoluble problems, a sea which, like Xerxes, we scourge with rods in an absurd attempt to punish it for what it has engulfed" (3:99-100; 3:104).

Hence, in the final pages of *La Prisonnière*, the narrative shifts gears to rise above the tumult of metaphors run amok into the stillness of allegory. Albertine is transformed into an awesome allegorical figure—"Allegorizing what? My death? My work?"[10]— both victim of and spelling defeat for the transgressor who has sought to capture and "redeem" her by force: great goddess of Time, winged Victory turned into a heavy slave, a figure of sleep and death, a Last Judgment: "It was indeed a dead woman that I saw when, presently, I entered her room. She had fallen asleep as soon as she lay down, her sheets, wrapped round her body like a shroud, had assumed, with their elegant folds, the rigidity of stone. It was as though, reminiscent of certain mediaeval Last Judgments, the head alone was emerging from the tomb, awaiting in its sleep the Archangel's trumpet" (3:366; 3:360).

Shortly before her flight, as he drives home with her from an outing in a bluish, moonlit night, the vision of the immobilizing power of abstraction is recapitulated in another key. The recapitulation lends added force to the text's suggestion that Albertine's fate is caused not only by the lover's destructive need to possess, but also by the impotence of the poet who has "recaptured" a fleeting reality in but a spectral image: "For the monuments of Paris had been substituted pure, linear, two-dimensional, a drawing of the monuments of Paris, as though in an attempt to recapture the appearance of a city that had been destroyed" (3:414; 3:407). Unlike Vermeer's little patch of yellow wall, life-redeeming and in the eyes of the dying Bergotte worth giving one's life for, or the divine round of the septet or the Proustian "sundial" itself, the abstract figure does not "sing." Contrary to its claim, it is born not of vision but of blindness; it is not a music which, without explaining, opens up and illuminates another's world, but a conceptual construct born of the poet's will to power.

No doubt the despair which impels the hero to freeze the beloved and hated image to free himself of her spell is a recurring *motif* of Proustian love and, as such, the opposite of the joy of authentic creation depicted by the cycle. But, as *La Prisonnière* keeps reminding the reader, all is double. The lover's and the artist's decipherings converge in an essential revelation which constitutes the other side of the "sundial:" the elusiveness of truth. Indeed, the situation of the narrator, unable to the very end of the cycle to begin his book, appears more closely akin to the blinded lover's torment than to the ancient seer's or medieval allegorist's bliss. When his object, which is to seize his life in its entirety in its essential truth, proves resistant to his design, as the beloved to the lover's, he too is in danger of seeking to subdue it by force, by confining it in the prison of abstraction.

If Albertine serves as the cycle's foremost embodiment of life's boundless exuberance, its opaqueness and unarrestable shifts, her death reflects the violence these may engender in the orphic lover and truth-seeker. To see in her merely the last beloved in the cycle, who sums up all who have come before her and her nameless, no longer significant successors, would be a misreading. She is at no point a "real" character like Gilberte, Odette, Mme de Guermantes, or any of the other love objects in *A la recherche*, all of whom continue to live and change long after their lovers' pursuit of them has come to an end. All are recuperated as living characters through the perspective of a double vision: the lover's blindness, but also the sundial's light. In their lovers' eyes, their image may expand to cover the entire universe in accordance with the mysterious geography of the heart which, under the pressure of jealousy's infinite need to know, expands to infinity. Each new revelation about their past, present, whereabouts, thoughts, associations or doings, may merely multiply for the lover the unanswered questions, make more impossible a unified perception of them. But in the book of hours' "magical simultaneity" they are also seen belonging to a cluster of identifiable and interrelated spheres of life, which gives them throughout their manifold metamorphoses a measure of coherence. Other characters may assume an allegorical dimension (not counting the narrator or allegorical reader whose role in the text is that of the text's "seedbed," its central registering and transcribing consciousness): Odette, at the end of *Du côté de chez Swann*, to become queen in the Garden of Woman, or Charlus, in *Le Temps retrouvé*, to become Prometheus Chained to the Rock of Pure Matter. But the individuality of these is so strongly designed that no allegorical figure can reduce or obliterate it. Albertine alone is seen only through the eyes of the hero in the depth of his obsession, which means that she is not seen at all. And since this lover is also the cycle's truth-seeker and writer of the book to come, whose passion it is to lay bare life's hidden laws, she becomes a paradigmatic figure of life's resistance to that presumption. Such is her radical "otherness," so impenetrable her mystery that, when to her misfortune and his own, he "captures" her in a twofold act of transgression, the psychological one of the lover and the formal one of the decipherer and composer of figural designs, he not only fails to redeem her but condemns her to death. So throughly and vengefully is she traduced into sleep and death,[11] that her "actual" accidental death in *La Fugitive* seems designed to exorcize all at once the lover's need for revenge and the danger of a transgression against life by the book to come.

5. A Book of Questions

True to its design, *La Fugitive* is less rich in figures than the volume of which it forms the counterpart. But like the other's, its title too serves as a powerful metaphor of its side of *A la recherche*'s decipherings. Not only Albertine, but all of life assumes in *La Fugitive* the face of a fugitive defying capture. To the orphic quester, this is life's sorrow. Yet, as he discovers also, it is not without a beauty of its own, since the undeciphered alone has the power to rekindle desire in him. It keeps the "stagnant reservoir" of the self,[1] and the pages of the book to come open to the continued influx of the unknown, forestalling their closure through a steady succession of shocks and surprises. To the book of hours' revelation of life's essential, abiding oneness within diversity, the cycle opposes, particularly in *La Fugitive*, diversity itself, irreducible and unfathomable, in the form of ever new and unassimilable hours. The figure of the sundial yields to that of the kaleidoscope whose continually shifting fragments refuse to hold together. It shows life as a perpetual disintegration and contamination of familiar forms, out of which strange new forms keep emerging,[2] carrying within them new riddles to be solved. The truth embodied in this side of the text is time's relentless power of metamorphosis and, hence, the distance separating everything in creation, including the truth-seeker's transcriptions, from the essential identity from which it appears debarred.

With the escape of Albertine, the unifying allegorical construct built around her in *La Prisonnière* falls apart. In a mixture of revenge and exuberance, life in *La Fugitive* seems bent on turning her death into an occasion for reasserting the reign of multiplicity, as "innumerable Albertines" invade the hero's consciousness to punish and torment him: "This disintegration does not only make the dead alive, it multiplies him or her. In order to be consoled, I would have to forget not one, but innumerable Albertines. When I had succeeded in bearing the grief of losing this Albertine, I must begin again with another, with a hundred others" (3:487; 3:478). Electrifying through pain his innumerable forgotten selves, they lead him to give her chase through innumerable moments, places and scenes of an irretrievable past, through innumerable young girls bearing a vague resemblance to her in a disorbited present and, through dream and word associations which add a new dimension of strangeness to the already strange, leading nowhere and clarifying nothing, compel his imagination to confront at last an intractable reality.

"We see, we hear, we conceive the world all wrong," is the text's plaintive *leitmotiv*. "We have of the universe only inchoate, fragmentary visions, which we complement by arbitrary associations of ideas, creative and dangerous illusions" (3:586; 3:574). In the world of *La Fugitive* which is multiple and heterogeneous to the core, misreading is no longer confined to the blindness of the lived moment, to be rectified by the book. No prescience, nor reminiscence, no penetrating metaphor can turn what appears to be pure, capricious chance into necessity. And so *La Fugitive*, in a daring poetic wager, is dedicated to the muse that speaks of time and metamorphosis and "of the vicissitudes of fortune," "the Muse that has gathered up everything that the more exalted Muses of philosophy and art have rejected, everything that is not founded upon truth, everything that is merely contingency, but that reveals other laws as well: the Muse of History" (3:692-693; 3:675).

However, in no way does this conversion turn *A la recherche* into a chronicle, at home as it were in time. Nor does the text really relinquish the "more exalted muses" of philosophy and art. The narrator's highest conscious aspiration remains to translate the "shimmering instability of the waves" into immutable laws. But the text's fidelity to this aspiration now takes the only form it can without falsely reducing to unity a decentered world of violent upheavals. It turns into a fictional kaleidoscope which captures the world's very resistance to being captured and makes visible its stubborn difference from what it might ideally be. Its task is no less compelling or poetic than the sundial's. What the kaleidoscope brings into view is both illuminating and deeply ambiguous: Is it life's abhorrence of truth as a laying bare of its secret springs, the basic evasiveness of all living things fearing intrusion, from rivers concealing their source to Albertine's defensive lies? Or is it that the innumerable signs which beckon to the decipherer and shock him with their strangeness defy his efforts simply because they contain no secret meaning? These questions neither the narrator nor the reader of *A la recherche* can answer with certainty. But what is certain is the force of disparity itself in all of life, including artistic creation in which every book must point towards a book always still to be written. Disparity is the only indisputable truth in

La Fugitive, and it keeps the volume spinning as none other in the cycle. A book of questions which does not cease to aspire to the status of a book of hours, it seems the strangest, most poignant and most profoundly modern of the cycle's volumes.

From its opening pages, as it spells out the lover's and truth-decipherer's defeat, *La Fugitive* bears witness to a new insight born of that defeat, namely, the knowledge of its not knowing, not being able to see through and beyond the opacity of life's ever changing constellations. Its plunge back into the realm of the indecipherable is evoked with an artfulness which creates the illusion of a metteur-en-scène's surrender, as in a "happening," to the strictly fortuitous and mystifying combinations and permutations of the moment. Metaphors and allegorical figures yield to a veritable litany of verbs, nouns and adjectives which make palpable the violence of life's perpetual dying, changing and dissembling: dissipate, disperse; disintegration, dissimilarity, profusion, proliferation; innumerable, successive, unknown, dissimilar, etc. In its whirling movement, everything—characters, places, thoughts, feelings and, most significantly, language too—disintegrates and becomes unrecognizable. Elucidation of analogies through metaphor yields to the contaminating power of "metastasis," of which the wonderfully absurd, Moliéresque exchange, in *Sodome et Gomorrhe*, between the hero, Brichot and Cottard that ensues from the learned professor's refutations of the curé of Combray's etymologies, has provided a foretaste:

> I protested that at Combray the curé had often told us interesting etymological dissertations.
>
> "He was probably better on his own ground, the move to Normandy must have made him lose his bearings."
>
> "Nor did it do him any good," I added, "for he came here with neurasthenia and went away again with rheumatism."
>
> "Ah, his neurasthenia is to blame. He has lapsed from neurasthenia into philology, as my worthy master Poquelin would have said. Tell us, Cottard, do you suppose that neurasthenia can have a pernicious effect on philology, philology a soothing effect on neurasthenia, and the relief from neurasthenia lead to rheumatism?"
>
> "Absolutely: rheumatism and neurasthenia are vicarious forms of neuro-arthritism. You may pass from one to the other by metastasis." (2:921; 2:891)

Metonymy has retreated from the sphere of the "higher muses," in which it can be transformed into metaphor,[3] to become the material of a poetry of the incongruous in which everything, from Pascal's *Pensées* to a soap commercial, can at least fleetingly become and be called anything, through the "metastases" of reality and of language. There are no more definitive origins or ends. Not only do the endless etymological explanations with which the curé of Combray used to wear out Aunt Léonie prove to be more than questionable, but in the distraught hero's readings—that sacrosant Proustian act of discovery—the simple name of the Buttes Chaumont turns up seemingly everywhere in a maze of metonymic, etymological and purely affective associations, which combine a great power to feed his obsession with Albertine with no power at all to shed light on the tormenting questions of whether or not, despite Albertine's denials, they were her and Andrée's favorite haunt and whether or not the girls' amusements there were innocent or lesbian games. So widely is the particular place name scattered in a burst of centrifugal dispersion, that it contaminates everything, is all at once nowhere and everywhere, and becomes as dangerous as it is fascinating in the unanswerable questions it brings to the fore:

> The fact is that from each of our ideas, as from a crossroads in a forest, so many paths branch off in different directions that at the moment when I least expected it I found myself faced by a fresh memory. The title of Fauré's melody *le Secret* had led me to the Duc de Broglie's *Secret du Roi*, the name Broglie to that of Chaumont; or else the words 'Good Friday' had made me think of Golgotha, Golgotha of the etymology of the word which is, it seems, the equivalent of *Calvus Mons*, Chaumont. But, whatever the path by which I had arrived at Chaumont, at that moment I received so violent a shock that I was far more concerned to ward off pain than to probe for memories. Some moments after the shock, my intelligence, which, like the sound of thunder travels less rapidly, produced the reason for it. Chaumont had made me think of the Buttes-Chaumont, where Mme. Bontemps had told me that Andrée used often to go with Albertine, whereas Albertine had told me that she had never seen the Buttes-Chaumont. (3:553; 3:543)

La Fugitive is a tale of revenge and reversal. He who has sought to weave a magic circle around his captive and make her the "fixed star" of an imaginary universe, finds himself caught in the whirling, multiple circles of a world that appears to have no center. Every lead that promises to bring him closer to the truth of

Albertine's life, from Andrée's first denials of a lesbian relationship with her friend to her subsequent admission of it and detailed, possibly slanderous descriptions of Albertine's orgies with little girls procured for her by Morel in the brothel for women at Couliville; from Aimée's terrible reports about the bathhouses of Balbec, to the discovery that Mme Verdurin's nephew, "Je suis dans les choux," had asked for Albertine's hand and might well have been the real cause of her eagerness to go to the Verdurins' on that evening when he suspected her of being eager only to resume her relationship with Mlle Vinteuil, each of these unexpected glimpses compounds the questions, opens up new, totally unexpected possibilities and takes him back to where he had started. Life, he discovers, ensnares the truth-seeker in a vicious circle. If it has a center, that center remains, and must be shown to remain, as elusive as the mysterious Campo in the labyrinth of narrow streets which, in the course of a nocturnal, "Arabian Nights" - like exploration of Venice, he believed to have discovered, only to find himself unable the next day to verify its reality: "The next day, I set out in quest of my nocturnal *piazza*, following *calle* after *calle* which were exactly like one another and refused to give me the smallest piece of information, except such as would lead me further astray. Sometimes a vague landmark which I seemed to recognize led me to suppose that I was about to see appear, in its seclusion, solitude and silence, the beautiful exiled *piazza*. At that moment, some evil genie which had assumed the form of a new *calle* made me unwittingly retrace my steps, and I found myself brought back to the Grand Canal" (3:665-666; 3:651).

All leads mislead. Abruptly, the discovery of the absence of a unifying truth makes a lie of knowledge. It restores to primacy those multiple, fragile realities of the body, subject to time and chance, which the "eternalizing" muses of philosophy and art have sought to *translate* into truth, and reveals them to *be* the truth. The innumerable small facts that make up life change face: from clues they turn into teasers. Every new little fact which comes into sight in the kaleidoscopic gyrations of *La Fugitive* tends to pull down a whole edifice of certainties, without furnishing the least new certainty to replace what it has destroyed. The eternalizing muse of *A la recherche* may say: ". . . is not a single small fact, if it is well chosen, sufficient to enable the experimenter to deduce a general law which will reveal the truth about thousands of analogous facts?" (3:524; 3:514) But the other muse, a hundred odd pages further on, offers this comment on Andrée's explanation of Albertine's abrupt departure from Balbec several summers earlier: "... there was this much truth in what Andrée said: if *differences* between minds account for the *different* impression produced upon one person and another by the same work, and *differences* of feeling for the impossibility of captivating a person who does not love you, there are also *differences* between characters, which are also motives for action. Then I ceased to think about this explanation and said to myself how difficult it is to know the truth in this world" (3:634; 3:620, my italics).

The spinning planet of Albertine's life becomes, as the narrative unfolds, but one of a multiplying number of planets all of which are marked by the same impenetrability. There is the multifaceted mystery of Gilberte in whom have so strangely combined the irreconcilable traits of Odette and Swann; her startling recognition after her father's death by the duc and duchesse de Guermantes who for years have denied their "dear Charles" the satisfaction of introducing her to them; her links with the world of Gomorrha; her marriage to Saint-Loup which flies in the face of the Faubourg Saint-Germain's most immutable taboos. Contiguous to her is the strange planet called Andrée in her not two nor three but multiple conflicting natures: friend and enemy; kind, destructive, and on a still deeper level kind again, sensitive and discriminating, yet who ends up marrying the "brute épaisse," Octave, whom the little band, herself included, appeared to despise but who, surprise piled on surprise, turns out to be not only an artist of true originality but also the adored former lover of Rachel, who had abandoned the actress for the not at all striking Andrée who thus, in turn, becomes a source of fascination and jealousy for her friend Gilberte who has never ceased living under the spell of her husband's former mistress. Or, second only to Albertine in the sheer multiplicity of his disparate selves, there is Robert de Saint-Loup who, from *A l'ombre des jeunes filles* on, has become more and more unfathomable to his friend, the hero, who believed he knew him. In the novel's continuous breaking up of seemingly stable constellations and creation of new ones, these multiple planets are as likely to converge as they are to touch fleetingly or clash violently. For the law that governs their conjunctions appears to be that of pure chance. In stark contrast to the figures of the sundial face of *A la recherche*, they reveal no deeper, essential coherence, which means that conjunctions deemed impossible not only are possible but occur constantly. Hence the shocks of surprise which keep the text bouncing back and forth, and which are designed to produce in both the narrator and the reader an alternation of dismay at the contamination of the most cherished values and beliefs, and delight at life's seemingly infinite inventiveness.

The climax of these shocks and the volume's biggest double *coup de théâtre*, in which all the diverse planets are drawn into an improbable convergence, comes with the news contained in the two letters which the hero and his mother read on the train on their return trip from Venice: the shocking *mésalliance* of Robert, purest of Guermantes, with the daughter of the former Odette de Crécy; and the even more unlikely, sad and wonderful union of Mlle d'Oloron, who is none other than the niece of Jupien, Charlus' friend, procurer and male brothel keeper, and the young marquis de Cambremer, son of one of the most ancient and snobbish families of the Breton nobility. The mournful causes of this latter alliance are vice on the one side—Charlus' dependence on Jupien and desire to serve him by bestowing on the young girl one of his nobiliary titles, and snobbery on the other—the Cambremers' eagerness to raise their modest social standing by strengthening their ties to the Guermantes. On both sides, vice and snobbery are abetted by shameful lying, namely, the deliberately spread rumor that the bride is the baron de Charlus' natural child. And yet, as the hero does not fail to perceive, corruption is only one aspect of these strange new combinations. At the same time that they seem to bespeak an irreversible process of deterioration, they also infuse new energies and, not inconceivably, new virtues into closed worlds that, without this influx, would be doomed to extinction. Thus the charm and delicacy of feeling of the young bride—who had long before been recognized by the hero's grandmother to have far greater personal distinction than the duc de Guermantes— might well have infused new blood and new virtues into the Cambremers' stultified clan, were it not for her death only weeks after the wedding—a death needed by the story-teller to toss together at her funeral, in a comedy of errors, all the disparate social and moral elements that have gone into this "combination:"
" 'It's the reward of virtue. It's a marriage from the last chapter of one of Mme Sand's novels,' said my mother. (It's the wages of vice, a marriage from the end of a Balzac novel," thought I.) (3:673; 3:658)

The sheer fortuitousness of these combinations makes it impossible to sort out vices from virtues. It also reduces even the most momentous events to happenings which might just as easily not have happened or happened differently. Their abruptness, "the accident of their sudden impact" depresses the hero, fills him with a "gloom as dismal as the depression of moving house, as bitter as jealousy." But they also absorb his attention. Like his grandmother, among whose greatest joys were life's surprises, an unexpected piece of news, an amusing detail,—"How surprised she would have been, how this would have amused her!" says his mother as they discuss the two pieces of news—he too, even in his disillusionment and graver than ever doubts about his vocation, is fascinated by the unexpected and inexplicable. As it removes into an even further distance the dreamed-of book of essences and universal laws, he is still quite unable to envision the role it will have to play in the book to come, but the reader of *La Fugitive* is left in no doubt.

The predominant tonality of *La Fugitive* may be mournful, the text suffused with a sense of loss and futility; yet paradoxically, as it forsakes the "higher muses" and becomes a poetic kaleidoscope in which all things disintegrate to recombine into new constellations, it opens up a mode of reading which makes up for what it loses in cognitive assurance by its power of de-familiarization. A new kind of "poetic sensation" is engendered, which is quite unlike that produced by a glimpse of a hidden correspondence which bestows on a particular object—a hawthorn blossom, an apple tree—a "higher" reality. It is the sense of wonder in face of the "other" side of truth, namely, that nothing is like anything else. Analogies are false, the hero is led to reflect, and so are novels which reduce the mystery of things by means of analogies and causal links, and thus cannot compare, he thinks, to dreams which, through their blithe disregard for any kind of rational sequence, make visible "those mysterious differences from which beauty derives." Everything is different, and therein alone lies truth. The effects of any single cause, let alone complex of causes, are so multiple that they defy being subsumed under a general law. The hero's own love for Albertine, which appeared to him in retrospect to be the very paradigm of love's aberrations, was, he now sees, quite different from other loves, for example, Swann's love for Odette: "For nothing ever repeats itself exactly, and the most analogous lives which, thanks to kinship of character and similarity of circumstances, we may select in order to represent them as symmetrical, remain in many respects contrasting" (3:509; 3:499).

The hero's despondency over his blindness, or the faultiness of analogies, is counterbalanced by a revivified attention to life's genius for dissembling in the at least threefold sense of concealing, lying and deferring ends, which he has come to recognize as part of its inscrutable metamorphoses. Joseph K.'s angry retort to the parable of the doorkeeper in *The Trial*, that the Law seems to raise lying to a universal principle, narrows a perception which in *A la recherche*, and especially in *La Fugitive*, is more powerful and original because it transcends the purely negative ethical implications of lying. Dissembling, in the Proustian text, may be morally reprehensible but, more importantly, it is evoked as a principle of creation which extends from the mysteries of first causes, ends and the nature of the human person, through the fictions of art, to the realm of human relationship, all the way down to the nature's own concealments of her generative processes. Dissembling serves to safeguard the process of metamorphosis itself, forestalling arrest and misappropriation, and it serves truth by making visible the distance which separates all living forms from their elusive identity.

In the striking reversal of its "sundial" reading of truth, the cycle can be read as a protracted game of hide and seek, in which not finding is the true fulfillment of the reader's quest. It restores depth to a world rendered flat and drab by the illusion of familiarity, and gives new "elasticity and vital energy" to the truth-seeker, whether lover, poet or both: "Wherefore the mediocre woman whom we are astonished to see them loving enriches the universe for them far more than an intelligent woman would have done. Behind each of her words, they feel that a lie is lurking, behind each house to which she says that she has gone, another house, behind each action, each person, another action, another person . . . . All this confronts the sensitive intellectual with a universe full of depths which his jealousy longs to plumb and which is not without interest to his intelligence" (3:632; 3:616-617).[4]

Despite its somber tale of deaths and disintegrations, the narrative of *La Fugitive* engenders a sustained excitement. On its pages, the death of every living figure, natural, human or social, and the completion of every artistic one, releases a profusion of free-floating elements which raise new questions and produce new combinations. An unforeseen fact demolishes a carefully wrought construct of desire and logic; the "too soon" or "too late" of a disclosure makes it impossible to fit it into a meaningful context; a name foresakes its bearer to designate an improbable successor; every near-certainty is left suspended by the thread of a "perhaps," "but on the other hand," "however," or "if," and forced by its very precariousness to reshuffle its parts, in a ceaseless striving for stability. Thus, what the text presents to its reader as its blindness is in fact its most innovative vision: the radical instability of life in which there are only singulars which "become," die, and are assimilated into new constellations. Legrandin's misappropriation of the title of comte de Méséglise may be shocking to those who have known him as Legrandin or those who still remember the title's ancient roots and rightful claimant, but this misappropriation, like all others in which *A la recherche* abounds, culminating in the "patronne" 's accession to the title of princesse de Guermantes, is revealed by the book of questions to be but a perfect instance of what the seeker of essences sees as "that perpetual error which is precisely 'life,'" and which the book is powerless to redeem. Its truth is confined to showing that nothing existing in time can lay claim to an abiding essence. The narrator's reflection on Gilberte's erroneous belief, after she has become the marquise de Saint-Loup, that the ancient name has now given her a definitive self and position, applies as well to any other entity, including the book to come. Not only must its multiple and shifting parts be composed, tuned and balanced again and again in order to hold together, but this continues to be true even after a work's completion. No creation will continue to "sing" if it is not continually recreated anew, which, in the case of the book, means read anew by each new generation of readers. "Everything that seems to us imperishable tends towards decay; a position in society, like anything else, is not created once and for all, but, just as much as the power of an Empire, is continually rebuilding by a sort of perpetual process of creation . . . . The creation of the world did not occur at the beginning of time, it occurs every day" (3:685-686; 3:669).

"Life is made up of a perpetual renewal of cells." As the tenuousness of the seemingly most stable, most complete entities comes to the fore, death and disintegration emerge in the novel as creation's prime movers. As in Baudelaire's "La Charogne," they release such a profusion of free "cells," that is to say, of new material for new compositions, that the hero, as the poet in the poem, is seized first by horror, then by an avid anticipation of rekindled creative passion. The "fixed star" of his love for Albertine explodes and is dispersed back into the "scattered dust of nebulae"; by the same token, love's metaphor, the little phrase of the sonata, having gone through its own process of "becoming," disintegrates back into its component elements: "When the little phrase, before disappearing altogether, dissolved into its various elements in which it floated still for a moment in scattered fragments, it was not for me, as it had been for Swann, a messenger from a vanishing Albertine.... I had been struck most of all by the elaboration, the trial runs, the repetitions, the gradual evolution of a phrase which developed through the course of my life" (3:571; 3:559-560). But decomposition seeds the ground for renewal: "Once again, as when I had ceased to see Gilberte, the love of women arose in me, relieved of any exclusive association with a particular woman already loved, and floated like those essences that have been liberated by previous destructions and stray suspended in the springtime air, asking only to be reunited with a new creature. Nowhere do so many flowers, 'forget-me-nots' though they be styled, germinate as in a cemetery" (3:572; 3:561).

Already in *La Prisonnière*, a few lines in the newspaper announcing the death of Swann—a death unexpected and suddenly brought home to the hero in its "striking and specific strangeness"—were sufficient to restore to him an aura of mystery lost years before, and to give rise in the hero's mind to "countless questions:"
"... countless questions occurred to me (as bubbles rise from the bottom of a pond) which I longed to ask him about the most disparate subjects: Vermeer, M. de Mouchy, Swann himself, a Boucher tapestry, Combray—questions which were doubtless not very urgent since I had put off asking them from day to day, but which seemed to me of cardinal importance now that, his lips being sealed, no answer would ever come" (3:200; 3:201).

Like Albertine, Swann has been freed by death from the misappropriations through which the decipherer's need to take hold of the unknown by reducing it to the known violates truth and also destroys his own deepest delight. In the narrator's awareness of this, the lover's error serves once again as a warning to the poet: "... in seeking to know Albertine, then to possess her entirely, I had merely obeyed the need to reduce by experiment to elements meanly akin to those of our own ego the mystery of every person, every place, which our imagination has made to seem different, and to impel each of our profound joys towards its own destruction" (3:509; 3:499).

That "profound joy" which makes itself felt in *La Fugitive* lies then not in deciphering, but rather in the intensely questioning attention called forth by a reality which remains steadfastly unassimilable in its difference. In contrast to the perfect sphere of its "sundial" face, whose recurring figures appear to capture and make transparent abiding human truths, *A la recherche* evokes in its "kaleidoscope" the impossibility of such closure. The narrative whirl of *La Fugitive*, first set in motion by the shock of Albertine's flight on the final pages of *La Prisonnière*, stops short as a new cluster of questions starts forming around a new Saint-Loup who is a total stranger now to the Saint-Loup who was once the hero's most admiring and solicitous friend, and flows over into the opening part of *Le Temps retrouvé*. To life's "perpetual error" it responds with a vertiginous round of questions which can only stop, but not end.

III.

Beyond the Text

6. Beyond the Text

Where does the end of *A la recherche* leave its hero? And where does it leave the reader? Since the two become linked in the metaphorical reader who emerges as the tale's major figure, the two questions are closely interrelated. Like the hero, the reader who has journeyed alongside him on his pilgrimage is left with no ultimate revelation to make his own. He is left instead with a powerful metaphor—in the form of a completed tale whose end is less a conclusion than a pointing towards a book yet to come—of a more than ever elusive truth which he in turn must continue to pursue.

Such is the tale's persuasiveness that its ending has persistently been read as ushering in the writing of *A la recherche du temps perdu*.[1] But is a *da capo* not precisely what it evokes as impossible? As Claude-Edmonde Magny put it brilliantly in linking the Proustian decipherer to Rilke's Orpheus, even when he has found his Eurydice, he can already no longer recognize her: she has become the root of things, reincorporated into the substance of the universe. Hence his search for her can never end.[2]

What could point up more sharply the essential character of the Proustian book as a book always still to come than the distance which separates the mother-text's seven-part perfection,[3] mirrored in the prism of Vinteuil's septet, from its hero's first tentative sketches that are vaguely mentioned at the cycle's end? It is the same distance which separates the weight, depth and permanence of the key figure of "Combray," the church of Saint-Hilaire, from the two fragile figures evoking the self's duration at the end: the fleeting image of Mlle de Saint-Loup and the sound of the little bell at aunt Léonie's garden gate. Unlike Saint-Hilaire whose spiritual truth hardly needs deciphering by the text, which on the contrary buttresses the text's revelations with a Gothic church's inherent spiritual presence, the "star"-like figure of the young girl is a purely immanent link between disparate seasons, born of time and contingency. It has no intrinsic power to "reveal" to the hero his self's essential identity. Like the sound of the bell finally heard again by the inner ear of memory, it can only summon him to compose that identity in an act of poetic self-creation. It is a strategic "transverse" thread, by means of which he hopes to be able to weave the labyrinthine "forest" of his life into a meaningful narrative constellation: "Was she not one of those star-shaped cross-roads in a forest whose roads converge from the most diverse quarters? Numerous for me were the roads which led to Mlle de Saint-Loup and which radiated around her" (3:1084-1085; 3:1029).[4]

At the completion of the cycle's final "Matinée" chapter, both the hero and the reader may well be back at the first stage of the creative progression "son - sonnette - sonate - vocare," noted by Georges Matoré and Irène Mecz,[5] but they begin anew in a universe which, in the course of the cycle's revolutions, has not ceased to shift before the hero's eyes and which has brought him to the realization that at every moment it "had to be totally redrawn."

Ostensibly, the cycle admits no hiatus between the completed tale and the book to come. As the promised book appears to emerge as a faint figure on the horizon, beginning and end appear to converge perfectly. As story time and narrative time converge, and with them the figure of Marcel the hero with that of the narrator and, by implication, the writer of *A la recherche du temps perdu*, so too, the tale implies, will the figural constellations of the book to come coincide with those of the mother-text, since both ostensibly transcribe the same inner cryptogram. Yet as the increasingly violent mutations of every figure in the text have shown, nothing remains the same. There can no more be a recapitulation of a text than a fictional protagonist who simply "repeats" the creative act of his progenitor. The very force of the latter, which transforms whatever it touches, makes it impossible.

A remarkable discrepancy is embedded in *A la recherche*'s depiction of the book's relationship to time, which a closer look at the hero and putative writer may serve to bring into clearer view. However Proust-like he may appear in a number of traits and experiences and in his way of seeing, the ideally evoked convergence between him and his creator must recede in the reader's mind before a first significant difference. Even from his earliest, least memorable years, Marcel Proust was a writer. He was a master composer who, in his relatively short, illness-plagued life, produced thousands of pages, ranging from the adolescent sketches of *Les Plaisirs et les jours* to the apprenticeship *Pastiches*, his first, later abandoned novel *Jean Santeuil*, the immediate precursor of *A la recherche*, *Contre Sainte-Beuve* and, finally, to the novel in which all previous texts would find their consummation. In stark contrast, his hero is a procrastinator who has kept postponing the act of writing from day to day and year to year, right to the threshold of old age where he can already see death awaiting him. The only writings with which the tale credits him directly, out of the vast store of Proust's own, are the translation of Ruskin's *Sesame and Lilies*, and that article in *Le Figaro* whose appearance takes on the dimensions of a major event in both *Contre Sainte-Beuve* and *La Fugitive*. In addition to these, the hero alludes vaguely in the "Matinée" chapter to other articles and to drafts of the first part of his book. In all, these would seem to add up to scant preparation for the composing of a work which he envisions as a new *Mémoires* of Saint-Simon, a new *Arabian Nights*, and which the reader, placing his faith in the cycle's final promise, assumes to be *A la recherche du temps perdu*. By the time we take leave of him, at the end of a tale which has traced an inordinately prolonged process of "reading" the endless and increasingly ambiguous signs which experience has inscribed in him, culminating in an anguished meditation on how to fit them all together, he appears so drained of creative vigor and confidence that it does indeed seem too late for him to begin.

"Was there still time?" "Was it not too late?" The narrator's anguish in face of the overwhelming complexity of his task evokes a frame of mind which one could liken, by substituting "begin" for "go on," to the protagonist's desperate resolve in Beckett's *L'Innommable*: ". . . I must begin, I can't begin, I must begin, so I shall begin . . ." If anything, his beginning appears more problematical than the other's going on which an uninterrupted flow of Beckettian texts has vouchsafed.

At first glance, the history of Proust's own writing of *A la recherche* might tend to dispel some of the doubt in which the narrator's book is shrouded. It is of course a known fact that the cycle's first chapter, "Combray," and the first draft of the final "Matinée" chapter, out of which, after a note of triumph, speaks that immense weariness in face of the difficulties ahead, were written first.[6] Still, the writer's weariness notwithstanding, the intervening volumes came out in a steady, unbroken succession. But the beginning and the end of the cycle are precisely the two parts of *A la recherche* in which the cycle's unity, its prophetic "translation" of life as a "sundial" of analogies and recurrence, is the most pronounced. In these initially conceived parts, its main lines are still uncluttered, its "constellations" a marvel of symmetry. But by the time the hero himself has reached the threshold of writing, it is more than twelve years and six volumes of *A la recherche* later. The cycle's basic two hemispheres—of existence lived blindly in time, and of the seer's totalizing retrospective vision of that existence, or time overcome—have lost their intitial clarity. His reflection about the noblest and seemingly stablest of all social constellations in his world, the Guermantes family, can be applied to the cycle's "sundial" vision as well: Time has exerted its chemistry on it: "This coterie.... had itself, in its innermost and as I had thought stable constitution, undergone a profound transformation." In the disorbited gyrations of the interpolated volumes, which culminate in the frenzy of the war years in the first part of *Le Temps retrouvé*, ruled over by a time turned Moloch, its "divine round" has, if not been superseded entirely in the hero's vision, at least become increasingly disrupted by "errant milky ways." Its immutable stars have had to yield to new, ephemeral stars whose brightness now lights up the nocturnal sky. Significantly these purely time-born "stars" are by no means evoked wholly negatively: they appear in the form of modern planes and searchlights which protect Paris from the enemy's death-dealing bombs with an efficacy the real stars cannot match: "Aeroplanes were still mounting like rockets to the level of the stars, and searchlights, as they quartered the sky, wafted slowly across it what looked like a pale dust of stars, of errant milky ways. Meanwhile the aeroplanes took their places among the constellations and seeing these new "stars" one might well have supposed oneself to be in another hemisphere" (3:828-829; 3:801-802).

By the opening of the final chapter, the hero has journeyed through a world, both inner and outer, which has been transformed beyond recognition. What he has seen in journeying through the *full* cycle, with its interior, ever expanding and, to the seeker of timeless constellations, ominous "errant milky ways," has perforce changed the cycle's original cryptogram. The reader can only surmise that *A la recherche*'s unique interweaving of two conflicting visions of the book, the one, a hermeneutic deciphering of life's essential coherence beneath change, the other, a new fictional constellation structured by its own, purely ordinal metaphors, was possible only because the powerful basic text of beginning and end expanded gradually outward from its core. It was thus able to assimilate new "constellations" and widening discrepancies, and to charge the gaps left open between its narrative panels with the promise of revelations yet to come. By contrast, the book to come benefits from no such initial grace. Its bearer is all too heavy with the knowledge of life's radical fortuitousness, even as he is unable to relinquish the orphic seer's dream.

The two distinct parts into which the "Matinée" chapter is divided place before the hero and the reader in their sharpest divergence yet the two truths about time which are reflected in the two visions of the book. Their conflict brings to mind Balzac's *Louis Lambert*. Louis Lambert, the "Pythagoras" of a twosome mockingly called "The Poet-and-Pythagoras" by their classmates, is Balzac's modern heir of the ancient philosopher of mathematics and music, seer of the "harmony of the spheres," inspirer of Plato and the neo-Platonic mystic tradition. A seeker of the unitive principle, he aspires to leave behind the illusory realm of time and multiplicity, to return to the true realm of ideas. The Pythagorean vision bears a close analogy to the hero's vision of his book to which he clings until the end and which is spelled out by him in his meditation in the Guermantes library. Through the power of the involuntary memory, of which time has proved to be the intermittent and fortuitous vehicle, the seer is promised accession to an extratemporal realm of truth which, through most of his existence, that self-same time has screened from his sight. Life with all its permutations has been but a dream, and now that the dreamer has at last been awakened, snatched from time's jaws by the three epiphanies which have in rapid succession resurrected the gold and azure of Venice, the sea of Balbec, and the mournful train ride which has brought him back to Paris, that truth lies within his grasp. His book will be a seer's act of anamnesia: "... surely then, if there exists a method by which we can learn to *understand* these *forgotten words* once more, is it not our duty to make use of it, even if this means *transcribing* them first into *a language which is universal* but which for that very reason will at least be *permanent*, a language which may make out of those who are no more, *in their truest essence, a lasting acquisition for the minds of all mankind*? And as for that law of change which made these loved words unintelligible to us, if we succeed at least in *explaining* it, is not even our infirmity transformed into strength of a new kind?" (3:941; 3:903; my italics).

First implicitly and at the end directly, the cycle evokes a vertical tripartite figure of time which, modeled on the stages of a mystical ascent, embodies three supposedly successive stages of the book's genesis. In the first stage, which lasts through nearly all of the writer's existence in the world, the immediate, blinding experiences of love and mundane pursuits, punctuated intermittently by "extra-temporal" moments, inscribe their signs in his inner sketchbook. This stage is followed by a second, rising as it were above the first in the cycle's last chapter, and sharply telescoped in time: it is the moment of illumination in which the seer glimpses the possibility of deciphering the totality of the cryptogram he has been passively recording. Finally, on the dizzying summit of both his years and the fullness of latent knowledge, he must forsake what is left him of life in order to transcribe that knowledge into a real book.

From the vantage point of the book to come, this is a strange, sad figure, announcing an unhappy ending. But it also bears little relation to time's actual role in the act of writing or any other form of composing as it is evoked in the cycle. No doubt the discoveries of unsuspected relationships between disparate phenomena by a Bergotte or Elstir are to an extent predicated on a past, made possible by involuntary memories, recurrences and new revelations, which enable the artist to recognize in retrospect analogies which he could not have grasped in the immediacy of a given moment. But at the same time his composings are also inseparably linked to the continuous process of living; they are not only contemporaneous with the successive stages of his life, but even anticipatory to the point where life itself will conform to its poetic prefiguration in the text, where "the poet will scarcely need to write, for he will be able to find in what he has already written the anticipatory outline of what will then be happening" (3:941-942; 3:904).

If "transcription" could begin only after life has been lived and is drawing to a close, there would be no books by the young Bergotte to enchant the adolescent hero, no sonata, no early Elstirs; above all, there would be no Proustian "sundial" to light up a thousand mysterious moments and create a universe overflowing with the promise of meaning. The reader's final glimpse of an aging, ill hero teetering over the chasm of the years and contemplating the task still awaiting him, can only confirm a truth which the text has throughout brought to the fore: the "reading" of life, in whatever form, is a continuous process of creation. It is not an illumination which suddenly overwhelms the writer with its demands upon him when time has just about run out.

And this truth unmasks the tale's most sustained sleight-of-hand whereby it depicts the hero's decipherings as a prelude to writing. For the writer, "reading" or deciphering does not precede writing, it *is* writing. Only by writing does he decipher life's truths, philosophical or poetic. The act of writing alone, with its continual discoveries and figural inventions, empowers him to compose a sustained figure of the world. Even reminiscence, as Gilles Deleuze has pointed out, becomes fully illuminating only when it is transformed into a metaphor that fastens the link between two similar moments.[7] Not the seer's mind, but the figures in the text disclose general laws if and where they can be discerned—such as the law which causes Gilberte de Saint-Loup's social decline as it had caused the decline of Oriane de Guermantes and, before her, the latter's aunt, the marquise de Villeparisis, namely, the twin tastes, so often inseparable in society women, "de s'instruire et de s'encanailler." More clearly yet, where there is only unfathomable difference, writing alone can compose it into a poetic truth. Out of the purely "transverse" links woven by time, and which in themselves have no power to give meaning to flux and disorder, it weaves a harmony of its own unlike any other, but yet, like *A la recherche*, so powerful in its intimation of what lies beyond it that it revolutionizes its reader's sense of reality. However persistently the tale evokes the book to come as born of memory, it discloses its own deeper truth: rather than composed retrospectively against time, and transcribing an order and meaning concealed by time, a book, even were it to be a messianic text, is composed prospectively, like Bergotte's novels or Vinteuil's chamber music, attuned to meanings still to emerge, and which it alone can call forth through the evocative power of its own design. Through the act of writing a "new star" comes into being, in whose particular light the closed, incommunicable world of an individual vision unlike any other becomes transparently meaningful to others; and simultaneously the writing self is transformed into a new self, its disparate "ways" composed and brought closer to their elusive identity. The text transforms the world it "reads" by the very act of its "reading," empowering it, in Michel Butor's words, to see itself in it, to be changed by it, and to see itself changing: "Proust's book, so closed in the beginning, so much a refuge against the world, becomes as it grows, and in particular through the medium of those basic stages of reflection that are its imaginary works of art, an open book in which the entire world must be able to see itself, . . . change, . . . and see itself changing."[8]

What then about the book to come? It too can only be a prospective creation, however large a role memory may play in it.

If *A la recherche*'s decipherings have indeed uncovered new questions and a world to be redesigned, these do await a new book. But will it be written by the hero? It seems unlikely. Not only does it seem too late for him but, since his "reading" throughout the cycle has in truth been Marcel Proust's writing, is he the one to write the new book that now demands to be written? His "readings" which demand it have been fully transcribed. What they call for is not a retranscription, but a new reading of the world they have transformed. The prospect opened up by the unfinished tale is not that of a *da capo*, but of a move beyond its pages, in which its hero and metaphorical reader yields his role to a reader no longer in, but rather of *A la recherche*, one who is a real writer and perhaps still young, and who will weave out of the "errant milky ways" inscribed in the cycle a new fictional design. As *A la recherche* wove imaginary works of art into its tale of a book to come to highlight the role of pre-texts in its genesis and, thus, to integrate it as visibly as possible into a continuous chain of creative filiations, he may weave actual fragments of *A la recherche*, or ironic permutations thereof, into his, as did for example Claude Simon in *La Bataille de Pharsale*,[9] and for an analogous purpose; namely, to bring to the fore the infinite mutability of elements which, when set free from their original context and seemingly clear-cut and intrinsic meanings, will combine in new ways to take on fresh meanings. Surely, we may say in the light of a number of works of post-Proustian fiction, the book to come will be a tale of Orpheus dismembered, in which "reading" will have taken on more decisively the meaning towards which the Proustian cycle has steered it. It will place its wager for truth less on a deciphering of life's coherence through memory and recognition, than on the shocks, the questions, the haunting sense of loss—the amnesiac's remembering only that he has forgotten—produced by the force inherent in each moment of time to explode familiar constellations and generate new ones. De-familiarizing the falsely familiar, the book to come will evoke each sign within its visual field not as a carrier of a predetermined meaning, but as a "conducting body"[10] moving towards and combining with other signs, to form a new textual constellation evoking a new meaning. The latter will appear, at least at first, inscrutable to the reader in the cognitive sense, but all the more will its power of appeal recharge two faculties in him which Blanchot has shown to be inseparable: his expectation (*attente*) and attention.

Conclusion

If *A la recherche* remains today for its readers, including those master readers, the novelists, the most illuminating of books, it is surely not because of its appeal to nostalgia. Rather, the crucial conflict that is inscribed in its tale of a book to come transformed it into so far-reaching an exploration of the possibilities and the limits of reading, that it is still pointing the way for them.

This conflict, played out in the mind of the cycle's protagonist, and embodied in the figures of Marcel Proust's text, pits against one another two visions of the book which are philosophically irreconcilable. The first, born of an orphic tradition given new life by the nineteenth century poet-seers who were among Proust's major precursors, promises the reader the possibility of bringing the world to light in its innermost truth as a "sundial" of essential, ever recurring hours and, hence, of delivering it from the illusion, wrought by time, that all of life is a matter of flux, chance, and irreducible multiplicity. Analogous to Balzac's ostensibly Swendenborgian vision of earth as the "seedbed of heaven,"[1] the tale told by *A la recherche du temps perdu* presents the totality of its hero's life as the seedbed of a book or, alternately, complementing this nature metaphor with a scriptural one, as a palimpsest of which every invisible layer and letter strives toward the book as its revelation and redemption. As the novel spins its tale, weaving together in the figurative "inner book" of its hero's self the myriad discrete moments, places and events of his life with those of history, biblical parable, myth, legend and dream, each element, thus freed from its specificity, takes on the character of an Open Sesame, guardian of and key to a hidden, "extra-temporal" meaning. The narrator envisions his book as the resurrected body of his life, an afterlife in the form of a prophetic text freed from the bonds of time and contingency. Affirming the power of consciousness embodied in language to gain and to yield access to truth, his book will be a seer's retrospective illumination of life as a sphere in which revolve the ever recurring, fundamental hours that mark man's quest for salvation.

Glorious myth of the book: But will it, can it be realized? Within the distance kept open in the cycle between the powerfully Proustian tale of what is to be a book of revelation, and the hero's own elusive book the delivery of which remains shrouded in doubt right through the end, the orphic vision is forced to question itself and to disclose the other side of its truth. Again and again, the ideally evoked transcription of a hidden providential design is slated to criss-cross with and to defer to the evocation of a disorbited world which, in the utter randomness of its shifts and turns, is more akin to a kaleidoscope. Throwing up ever new and strange constellations to it for ever new and impossible decipherings, the latter disrupts the sundial's harmony and prevents the cycle's closure. How many of the hero's efforts to comprehend—in the two-fold sense of understanding and capturing—a sign's elusive meaning in the form of a metaphor or general law merely confront him more sharply with an enigma! Time and again signs which seem to be pleading to be deciphered refuse to yield up their secret, not just on those occasions when lack of will or circumstances prevent him from furnishing the necessary effort of concentration, as in the episode of the trees of Hudisménil, but even when his efforts are those of a man going under whose salvation, like a jealous lover's, depends on his discernment of the truth. As Marcel Proust's text kept proliferating in those thirteen years during which he worked on it, opening out, extending itself further and further in quest of an elusive totality in which not a thread would be left untied, its bulging inserts barely held together by Céleste Albaret's gluing skills, so his cycle's truth-seeker, in "reading" his inner book, is drawn more and more deeply into a labyrinth of questions and conjectures, impelled to pile metaphor on metaphor, "soit que" on "soit que," in a hopeless endeavor to give to each sign all the *possible* meanings it seems to invite. Indeed his blindness is not unlike the lover's. Repeatedly an Orpheus as lost as Swann in pursuit of his Eurydice around a spectral Champs-Elysées, or gazing in torment in the night at the "precious manuscript" of her window streaked with bars of light on the rue La Pérouse,[2] he appears fated to see his own Eurydice elude him, not only in the figure of Albertine, the fugitive beloved but, more importantly, in the figure which, though depicted as radically antithetical to her, emerges as intimately linked to her, his dreamed-of book.

The narrator's impulse to charge the least element of his life with a maximum of significance, to overcome its singularity by drawing it into an ever expanding network of analogies, is no doubt the most explicit and persistent *motif* in *La Recherche*. But, as if the very intensity of the Proustian quest for extra-temporal identities and general laws engendered its opposite, a contrary impulse can be seen steering the seer's "reading" continually back to the unevennesses and discrepancies in the dense surfaces of the concrete world, to the point where it is simply never done with them. The counterpart or double engendered by the book of hours is an open book of questions. From a euphoric vision of timeless, universal analogies underlying life's most disparate moments and linking them in near-identity, or of general laws to be uncovered underneath its reckless disorder, such as the law of heredity which at the end of Saint-Loup's life prevails and "frees" him as it were from the aberrations and idiosyncrasies of his successive selves to reveal him as a "pure Guermantes,"[3] the hero and the reader are drawn back into the thick of unsolved riddles. What is this finally revealed identity, a pure Guermantes? the reader wonders. What do Saint-Loup and his aunt, Oriane de Guermantes, have in common beyond the formal codes of their clan? Or the two brothers? Far more compelling than this questionable essence called Guermantes are the mysterious transformations which time has produced in Saint-Loup and which the hero's "reading" can only hold up to view in the form of questions: was his friend's passion for the sexually ambiguous Rachel an early sign of his later homosexuality? Or did he indeed love only women at the time of his friendship with the hero at Balbec and change later? But then again, what about the lift-boy, or his thrashing of the passer-by who accosted him on the street? These and innumerable other unanswered questions reverberate in the reader's mind, keeping the figure of Saint-Loup alive for him with a force that the pure Guermantes Robert is said to have become in his death cannot match.

Unlike Racine who could still offer his readers an "Angel's Bread" in his *Cantiques spirituelles*, a text echoing the word of God, and whom Proust emulated with self-mocking irony,[4] the writer of the book to come discovers, and warns his readers, that even the most beautiful of books can do no more than ask questions. In contrast to biblical and classical metaphors, rooted in and reflecting a divinely established truth, its own metaphors are *only* metaphors, that is, figures designed to, but both ontologically and cognitively powerless to bridge the gap between a bitterly felt absence of being and its passionately invoked presence. All too many of the figures which the hero "reads" in his inner book and with which *La Recherche* weaves the design of his life, evoke in the end an indeterminate truth which never stops shifting. Within the cycle's fictional space they disrupt the sundial to create, as in a Cubist field of force, a superior disequilibrium by means of a virtually limitless diversity of relationships, each of which both complements and subtly subverts all the others.[5]

The truth of the seer's powerlessness to see, brought to the fore by the book of questions, is the other, contemporary side of the Proustian tale's presentation of the book as truth-quest and orphic revelation. Already Jean Santeuil's reflections before the Monets of the Marquis de Réveillon made clear the quest's two-sidedness, its deciphering of truth and the truth of the world's ultimate indecipherability, which Impressionism had first made visible to the writer:

> Here it is already the river, but the eye is arrested, one no longer sees anything but a void, a fog which prevents one from seeing farther. In that part of the canvas one must paint neither what one sees, since one sees nothing, nor what one doesn't see, since one must paint only what one sees; but to paint that one doesn't see, that the deficiency of the eye unable to float over the fog is inflicted on the eye on both the canvas and the river, that is beautiful. And when it is a cathedral, that too is beautiful, since the portal one does not see is a beautiful thing and something which lives in nature. Certain hours of our life are beyond seeing, covered by fog and beyond anyone's grasp, and those hours too are beautiful.
> (JS, 896-897)

The cycle's extraordinary feat of interweaving its two key figures of the world to be "translated" by the book, the sundial and the kaleidoscope, does two things. It tempts the reader to seek in the book a transcendent revelation of life, in which he can find salvation from the anguish and falsehoods of existence. And at the same time it forbids him to read it as a messianic text. By concealing at least several riddles in nearly every truth it discloses, it propels his imagination beyond its own confines. Acknowledging the finiteness of its own, unique reading of life, and concomitant blindness to what lies outside and beyond its field of vision, it retains something of the mystery and incompleteness of life and thus becomes in its turn a new pre-text for new readings and new books.

But the unmasking of its allegory of the book as an uncovering of essences and identities makes visible another secret interplay. Everywhere around him, in every sphere of life, the hero discerns another pursuit which has little directly to do with a truth-quest in the hermeneutical sense, but in the marvelously variegated examples of which he nonetheless recognizes all-important prefigurations of his own book to come. What they teach him is not a seer's reading, but an artist's weaving of new constellations out of the contiguous threads of a radically immanent reality. The passion which underlies these creations is not in any direct sense the need to know, even though it proves itself to be a powerful ally of truth in its own right. Rather it is the creator's urge to give to the face of the world a coherence lacking in it through the force of his own design. His figures do not translate an already existing, albeit hidden, order; they create a new order and with it a new way of seeing. To the truth-seeker's distrust of time and his quest to uncover retrospectively ideas and essences which time has concealed, the poet responds with a concentrated attention to the moment's singularity and by drawing its very distinctiveness into a new harmony. Throughout the cycle's fictional universe—that same universe which the tale depicts as lost in error and headed toward death and oblivion—a chain of creative revisions extends from the "blind" artistic impulses of nature through the ephemeral or at best seasonal compositions of a Françoise or Odette to the imaginary masterpieces of its artists. In all of these the hero discerns the same striving: to translate the fortuitous phenomena of existence and their haphazard conjunctions into a meaningful, "necessary" whole. None of the multiple compositions which the tale inscribes in the hero's inner book as signposts guiding him toward his vocation, can claim to be truth in the messianic sense. But each, from the humblest to the most complex and compelling, embodies a fresh intimation of a heterogeneous world made whole and consonant. What they suggest, in defiance of the tale's explicit assertions, is that the book to come can be no more than one among them, however high a status its orphic aspiration may bestow on it. All the while—through the cycle's three thousand odd pages—that the hero's imagination is at work, building, weaving, cooking, sewing his cathedral - tapestry - boeuf à la mode - dress - novel, the reader is drawn into a continuous creative process which reveals as false the tale's staunchly upheld antithesis of book and life, and which steers him beyond the cycle's final pages back into a reality which the pages he has just finished reading have transformed and which must already be redrawn anew:

> And there, indeed, is one of the great and marvelous characteristics of beautiful books..., Proust wrote as early as 1905 in "Sur la lecture," that by the author they could be called "Conclusions" and by the reader "Initiations." We feel very clearly that our wisdom begins where that of the author ends, and we would like him to give us answers, when all he can do is give us desires. And these desires he can arouse in us only by making us contemplate the supreme beauty which the last effort of his art has allowed him to reach. But by a singular and, moreover, providential law of mental optics (a law which perhaps signifies that we can receive the truth from no one, but must create it ourselves), that which is the end of their wisdom appears to us but the beginning of ours, so that it is at the moment when they have told us all they could tell us that they create in us the feeling that they have told us nothing yet.[6]

Spanning the chasm between its Romantic legacy and the post-modern imagination, *A la recherche* is all at once modern fiction's last great romance of the book as a prophetic text, and that romance's transformation into an open book of questions and a poet's prospecting of a new world.

NOTES

Introduction

[1] This was the original title of Proust's preface to his translation of Ruskin's *Sesame and Lilies*, first published separately in the review *Renaissance latine* in 1905. It can now be found as "Journées de lecture" in *Contre Sainte-Beuve, précédé de Pastiches et mélanges et suivi de Essais et articles*, ed. Pierre Clarac et Yves Sandre (Paris: Ed. de la Pléiade, Gallimard, 1971), and its English translation, *On Reading*, by Jean Autret and William Burford, with an Introductory Note by William Burford (New York: The Macmillan Company, 1971).

[2] Marcel Proust, *Remembrance of Things Past*, tr. C. K. Scott Moncrieff and Terence Kilmartin; and by Andreas Mayor, 3 vols. (New York: Random House, 1981), 3:585; *A la recherche du temps perdu*, texte établi par Pierre Clarac et André Ferré, 3 vols. (Paris: Ed. de la Pléiade, Gallimard, 1954), 3: 573. This study is of course based on the original French text. For the convenience of English-speaking readers of Proust, I have used the Scott Moncrieff-Kilmartin translation for the phrases or passages I quote from the novel. For readers who are familiar with *A la recherche* in the original, each reference to the Random House edition is immediately followed by the reference to the French edition. However, I have kept the French titles of the cycle and its individual volumes in both the text and the notes. The French titles of the seven volumes of *A la recherche* and their English counterparts are: *Du côté de chez Swann - Swann's Way, A l'ombre des jeunes filles en fleur - Within a Budding Grove, Le côté de Guermantes - The Guermantes Way, Sodome et Gomorrhe - Cities of the Plain, La Prisonnière - The Captive, La Fugitive - The Sweat Cheat Gone, Le Temps retrouvé - The Past Recaptured*. All English translations from Proust's other works or other French texts are my own unless otherwise indicated.

[3] *Recherche*, 3: 1104; 3: 1046.

I. Pre-texts

1. Reading: Reality and Metaphor

[1] Margaret Mein, *A Foretaste of Proust: A Study of Proust and His Precursors* (Westmead, Fanborough, Hants: Saxon House, 1974).

[2] "There is no better way to become conscious of what we ourselves feel than to try to recreate in ourself what a master has felt. In that profound effort, it is our own thought which we bring to light, together with his." *Pastiches et mélanges*, 140. For the most comprehensive treatment of the role of books in Proust's evolution as a writer, see René de Chantal's *Marcel Proust, critique littéraire*, 2 vols. (Montréal: Les Presses de l'Université de Montréal, 1967).

[3]*Contre Sainte-Beuve*, préfacé de Bernard de Fallois (Paris: Gallimard, 1954), 268-291.

[4]*On Reading*, 39; "Journées de lecture," 178.

[5]Marcel Proust, *Jean Santeuil*, précédé de *Les Plaisirs et les jours*, ed. Pierre Clarac et Yves Sandre (Paris: Ed. de la Pléiade, Gallimard, 1971), 269.

[6]*Recherche*, 1:93-94; 1:87. Paul de Man, in "Reading (Proust)," in *Allegories of Reading: Figural Language in Rousseau, Nietzsche, Rilke and Proust* (New Haven and London: Yale University Press, 1979), allows for less intrinsic truth in this figure. Postulating a to me questionable polar opposition between mobility and immobility and inside and outside, he sees in their reconciliation in the figure of the fountain a key example of a figural strategy which creates a seductive but false, because purely textual, totalization of experience. Yet, as this study attempts to show, even where metaphor in *A la recherche* is more clearly a rhetorical artifice than it may be in this instance, the text still defies the categorizing of many of its figures as true or false in either the ontological or the epistemological sense. *A la recherche* not only has a correction built into its truth claim for the revelations of its hero's book to come in the form of an open book of questions. It further accentuates the distance separating the book from messianic truth by evoking it as part of a chain of artisanal and artistic compositions which can lay no claim to the power of naming Being in its fullness, but which have nevertheless a vital role to play in man's quest for that fullness and, hence, their own mode of truth which differs from that of the messianic text.

2. Threshold Creations

[1]Eugène Delacroix, *Journal*, 3 vols. (Paris: Plon, 1932).

[2]Georges Poulet, *L'Espace proustien* (Paris: Gallimard, 1963), 34-35.

[3]"Nature is only a dictionary, he often used to say." Charles Baudelaire, "L'Oeuvre et la vie d'Eugène Delacroix," *Oeuvres complètes*, 2 vols. Texte établi, présenté et annoté par Claude Pichois (Paris: Gallimard, 1976), 2:747.

[4]George Stambolian, *Marcel Proust and the Creative Encounter* (Chicago and London: The U. of Chicago Press, 1972), 129-130.

[5]See "Le Chant des sirènes," *Le Livre à venir* (Paris: Gallimard, 1959). Even though this essay's concern, which is to bring into focus the positive interplay in *A la recherche* between the book and the realities of lived experience, runs counter to Blanchot's vision of the book as annulling life, the latter's *néantisation*, I am deeply indebted to Blanchot's thought. Indeed it was largely in reaction to its impact that I felt prompted to attempt to show the "other side."

[6]Georges Poulet, "Proust," *Etudes sur le temps humain* (Paris: Plon, 1950).

[7]Poulet, "Proust," *Mesure de l'instant* (Paris: Plon, 1968). See also Georges Cattaui, *Proust et ses métamorphoses* (Paris: Nizet, 1972), 13: "If he recaptured time, it was not to restore the past, but to inaugurate the future."

3. A Ray of Sunlight

[1]I am indebted to Shoshana Felman for her demonstration of the link between the cognitive venture and the love quest in *Le Scandale du corps parlant: Don Juan avec Austin ou la séduction en deux langues* (Paris: Seuil, 1980).

[2]See for example Victor Brombert's reading in *The Romantic Prison: The French Tradition* (Princeton: Princeton U. Press, 1978).

[3]There have been a number of psychocritical studies on the dynamics of Proustian desire, its repression and displacements. See for example Jean Doubrovsky's *La Place de la madeleine* (Paris: Mercure de France, 1974). Their concern is too different from mine for me to have found them helpful. As Leo Bersani pointed out, rightly, I believe, in the Introduction to his *Marcel Proust: The Fictions of Life and Art* (London, Oxford, New York: Oxford U. Press, 1965), they have tended to shift the emphasis back, in neo-Beuvian fashion, from the text to a concern with the man *through* his life and work.

[4]See J. E. Cirlot on the psychological and mythological ambivalence of the volcano, its power of both destruction and creation: "As a psychological symbol, the volcano represents the passions which, according to Beaudoin, become the sole source of our spiritual energy once we have managed to master and transform them." *A Dictionary of Symbols* (New York: Philosophical Library, 1962), 342. Maurice Blanchot speaks of those moments in which the writer no longer knows whether he is remembering or inventing as moments which open up to him "the secret of becoming," as "cette secousse et cette fulguration où la liberté s'embrase, à la lumière de la conscience qui, un instant, la découvre." *L'Amitié* (Paris: Gallimard, 1971), 157-158.

[5]Charles Baudelaire, "Salon de 1859," *Oeuvres complètes*, 2:619-623.

[6]See *Recherche*, 3:937-938; 3:900-901n.

[7]See *L'Espace proustien*, in which Poulet's perception of the creative inner space in which Proustian experience composes itself shifts from the inner space of the mind to the volume or inner space of the text.

[8]Jean-Paul Sartre, *Being and Nothingness*, tr. and with an Introduction by Hazel E. Barnes (New York: Philosophical Library, 1956), 86.

[9]Sartre, 103.

[10]See Jean-Pierre Richard's analysis of the "duplicity" of the Proustian hermeneutic object in *Proust et le monde sensible* (Paris: Seuil, 1974), 134.

[11] This exchange is rooted in what Richard calls the Proustian principle of non-demarcation.

[12] Baudelaire, "Tableaux parisiens," *Oeuvres complètes*, 1:82, 83.

[13] In *A l'ombre des jeunes filles*, Bergotte acknowledges his admirers' enthusiasm for his books with great modesty, but "the instinct of the maker, the builder, was too deeply implanted in Bergotte for him not to be aware that the sole proof that he had built both usefully and truthfully lay in the pleasure his work had given, to himself first of all and afterwards to his readers." 1:599; 1:556. On the happiness of artistic creation in Proust, see also Henri Bonnet's *L'Eudémonisme esthétique de Proust* (Paris: Vrin, 1949).

[14] *Le Livre à venir*, 35.

II. The Text: Two-in-One

[1] On anxiety as "the most fertile ground from which allegorical abstractions appear," see Angus Fletcher, *Allegory: The Theory of a Symbolic Mode* (Ithaca and London: Cornell U. Press, 1964), especially ch. 1, "The Demonic Agent," and ch. 6, "Psychoanalytic Analogues: Obsession and Compulsion."

4. A Book of Hours

[1] Georges Cattaui, 282.

[2] Søren Kierkegaard, *Repetition*, tr. with an Introduction and Notes by Walter Lowrie (New York, Evanston and London: Harper Torchbooks, 9164), 33, 34.

[3] On the universal repetition compulsion or what Proust calls self-plagiarism, see *Recherche*, 3:443; 3:436.

[4] On Proustian prescience and reminiscence, see also Georges Piroué's *Proust et la musique du devenir* (Paris: Editions Denoel, 1960), especially 165: "... c'est une réminiscence qui n'accouche de rien d'autre que de sa propre forme, que de la qualité dont elle revêt toute chose. C'est un futur toujours renaissant qui détermine un passé toujours en gésine d'un certain futur, et ceci jusqu'à la consommation des temps." See also Roger Shattuck's excellent treatment of Proustian recognition, the alternate, more active and more permanent form of memory—and which, through its "stereoscopic vision," gives depth and unity to the figures it captures in their successive incarnations. Roger Shattuck, *Proust's Binoculars* (London: Chatto and Windus Ltd., 1963).

[5] Maurice Blanchot, "L'Expérience de Proust," *Le Livre à venir*, 21.

[6] On this double rotation, also on the allegorical dimension of *A la recherche*, see especially Georges Cattaui's *Proust et ses métamorphoses*.

[7] Claude-Edmonde Magny, in stressing the subjective character of the hero's allegorical journey, preferred to call it, using Schelling's term, a "tautegorical tale," that is, "a tale signifying nothing but itself, in the manner of Kafka's *Castle*, and not allegorical like the *Roman de la Rose* or Bunyan's *Pilgrim's Progress*." *Histoire du roman français depuis 1918* (Paris: Seuil, 1950), 152.

[8] The plane's vertical ascent becomes a metaphor for the demiurgic creations of a Wagner or Vinteuil. See 3:159; 3:162:
> Perhaps, as the birds that soar highest and fly most swiftly have more powerful wings, one of these frankly material vehicles was needed to explore the infinite, one of these 120 horsepower machines—brand-name Mystère—in which nevertheless, however high one flies, one is prevented to some extent from enjoying the silence of space by the overpowering roar of the engine!

[9] Walter Benjamin likens Albertine in black to Baudelaire's unknown woman in "A une passante," object of a love possible only in the city and of which "one might . . . say that it was spared, rather than denied fulfillment." "On Some Motifs in Baudelaire," *Illuminations*, edited and with an Introduction by Hannah Arendt, tr. by Harry Zohn (New York: Schocken Books, 1969), 170.

[10] 3:367; 3:360. Kilmartin has retained Scott Moncrieff's translation of the last noun as "love." Note the correction of the Pléiade edition's faulty "amour" to "oeuvre" by Alison Winton in her *Proust's Additions: The Making of "A la recherche du temps perdu*," 2 vols. (Cambridge, London, New York, Melbourne: Cambridge U. Press, 1977), 2:163.

[11] For a corroborative analysis of the narrator's temptation to kill reality, to make of it "something dead," removed from life, over which he can establish his reign, see Gaetan Picon's *Lecture de Proust* (Paris: Gallimard, 1963), 107-108. See also David R. Ellison's *The Reading of Proust* (Baltimore: Johns Hopkins University Press, 1984). This study appeared after mine was completed. Although it is a very different kind of book, some of its insights closely parallel my own.

5. A Book of Questions

[1] Leo Bersani's studies have focused especially on the creative self's need to venture out into worlds of the non-self in seeking to constitute its own truth, a truth no longer conceivable as essential and unitary, but having to be created continually out of multiple, shifting fragments.

[2] See Harry Levin: ". . . not without warrant, he himself adduces Ovid's *Metamorphoses*; and though he does not specifically mention Picasso, he cannot see an object or situation without envisioning a Cubist sequence of past and future states, of growth and wane, renewal and decomposition." *The Gates of Horn: A Study of Five French Realists* (New York: Oxford U. Press, 1963), 430.

[3] See Gérard Genette's analysis of the metonymic basis of many of Proust's metaphors in "Métonymie chez Proust," *Figures III* (Paris: Seuil, 1972).

[4] For a superb analysis of concealment as inherent in truth, see Jean Starobinski's prefatory essay, "Le Voile de Poppée," in *L'Oeil vivant* (Paris: Gallimard, 1961).

6. Beyond the Text

[1] I believe that Germaine Brée was the first critic to note that the cycle's complexity "blurs—in her words—the relationship between the genesis of the narrator's novel (a novel which is never written), the theory of the novel which he expounds, and the book which Proust himself has written." *Marcel Proust and Deliverance from Time* (New Brunswick: Rutgers University Press, 1955), 219.

[2] *Le Roman français depuis 1918*, 198.

[3] See J. E. Cirlot on the number seven in *A Dictionary of Symbols:* "Symbol of perfect order, a complete period or cycle. It comprises the union of the ternary and the quaternary, and hence it is endowed with exceptional value . . . . It is the number forming the basic series of musical notes, of colours and of the planetary spheres as well as of the gods corresponding to them; and also of the capital sins and their opposing virtues. It also corresponds to the three-dimensional cross and, finally, it is the symbol of pain." 223.

[4] Jean Ricardou, in "Proust: A Retrospective Reading," *Critical Inquiry*, Spring 1982, 531-547, sees in Proust's metaphors forerunners of what he calls the "ordinal metaphors" of the New Novel. They are not representative or expressive, but productive. Their function is to organize the narrative order.

[5] Georges Matoré and Irène Mecz, *Musique et structure romanesque dans la "Recherche du temps perdu"* (Paris: Klincksieck, 1972).

[6] See Bernard Brun's "*Le Temps retrouvé* dans les avant-textes de 'Combray,' " in *Bulletin d'Informations proustiennes*, no. 12, 1981 (Paris: Presses de l'Ecole Normale Supérieure, 1981), 14.

[7] Gilles Deleuze, *Proust et les signes* (Paris: Presses Universitaires de France, 1971), 68.

[8] Michel Butor, "Les oeuvres d'art imaginaires chez Proust," *Essais sur les modernes* (Paris: Gallimard, 1960), 197.

[9] *La Bataille de Pharsale* (Paris: Editions de Minuit, 1969); *The Battle of Pharsalus*, tr. by Richard Howard (New York: George Braziller; London: Jonathan Cape, 1971).

Gerda R. Blumenthal

[10] See Claude Simon, *Les Corps conducteurs* (Paris: Editions de Minuit, 1971); *Conducting Bodies*, tr. by Helen R. Lane (New York: Viking Press; London: Calder-Boyars; Canada: The Macmillan Company of Canada, 1974).

Conclusion

[1] Honoré de Balzac, *Séraphita, La Comédie humaine*, texte préfacé et établi par Marcel Bouteron, 10 vols. (Paris: Gallimard, 1962), 10:505.

[2] *Recherche*, 1:299; 1:274.

[3] 3:881-882; 3:851:
And this Guermantes had died more himself than ever before, or rather more a member of his race, into which he slowly dissolved until he became nothing more than a Guermantes, as was symbolically visible at his burial in the church of Saint-Hilaire at Combray, completely hung for the occasion with black draperies upon which stood out in red, beneath the closed circle of the coronet, without initials of Christian names or titles, the G of the Guermantes that he had again in death become.

[4] *Essais et articles*, 604-605. An interviewer asked: "What would you do if you were forced to do manual work?" Proust, after taking him to task for making too sharp a distinction between mental and manual work, replied: "You will allow me to base my answer on the collaboration of mind and hand and tell you that if I were in the situation you describe, I would take as a manual job exactly the one I am practicing right now, writing. And if there were absolutely no paper to be had, I think I would become a baker. It is honorable to give men their daily bread. In the meantime I produce as best I can that 'Angel's Bread' of which Racine (whom I am quoting from memory and no doubt inaccurately) said:
    Dieu lui-même le compose
    De la fleur de son froment.
    C'est ce pain si délectable
    Que ne sert pas à sa table
    Le monde que vous suivez.
    Je l'offre à qui veut me suivre:
    Approchez. Voulez-vous vivre?
    Prenez, mangez et vivez!
Don't you think that here Racine resembles M. Paul Valéry a little, who rediscovered Malherbes via Mallarmé?"

[5] Gabriel Josipovici, in *The World and the Book* (New York: The Macmillan Company, 1971), speaks of the modern "demon of analogy." Max Kosloff's discussion of Cubist space in *Cubism/Futurism* (New York: Charterhouse Press, 1973) was very helpful to me.

[6] *On Reading*, 35-36; "Journées de lecture," 176-177.